NAKED

The girl, Tia, had offered Skye Fargo an invitation too enticing to turn down. Now she lay naked in the hay as he headed out the barn door to take a break, silencing her protests by promising a fast return.

It would be a hard promise to keep.

A man's voice snarled, "You caused my kid brother to be killed."

Fargo flattened his back to the wall. Pete Miller sat astride a horse, aiming a big revolver at Fargo's broad chest.

Skye stood there, helpless, with his gun belt off and his life on the finish line as the ruthless killer growled, "*Adios*, you big son of a bitch."

THE
TRAILSMAN
117

GUN
VALLEY

by

Jon Sharpe

A SIGNET BOOK

SIGNET
Published by the Penguin Group
Penguin Books USA Inc., 375 Hudson Street,
New York, New York, 10014, U.S.A.
Penguin Books Ltd, 27 Wrights Lane, London W8 5TZ, England
Penguin Books Australia Ltd, Ringwood, Victoria, Australia
Penguin Books Canada Ltd, 2801 John Street,
Markham, Ontario, Canada L3R 1B4
Penguin Books (N.Z.) Ltd, 182-190 Wairau Road,
Auckland 10, New Zealand

Penguin Books Ltd, Registered Offices:
Harmondsworth, Middlesex, England

First published by Signet, an imprint of New American Library,
a division of Penguin Books USA Inc.

First Printing, September, 1991

10 9 8 7 6 5 4 3 2 1

The first chapter of this book originally appeared in *Kansas Kill*,
the one hundred sixteenth volume in this series.

 REGISTERED TRADEMARK—MARCA REGISTRADA

PRINTED IN THE UNITED STATES OF AMERICA

The Trailsman

Beginnings . . . they bend the tree and they mark the man. Skye Fargo was born when he was eighteen. Terror was his midwife, vengeance his first cry. Killing spawned Skye Fargo, ruthless, cold-blooded murder. Out of the acrid smoke of gunpowder still hanging in the air, he rose, cried out a promise never forgotten.

The Trailsman they began to call him all across the West: searcher, scout, hunter, the man who could see where others only looked, his skills for hire but not his soul, the man who lived each day to the fullest, yet trailed each tomorrow. Skye Fargo, the Trailsman, the seeker who could take the wildness of a land and the wanting of a woman and make them his own.

Fall, 1860, in Arizona Territory,
where a band of killers left
a trail of human blood until they
met the devil himself in a
place called Gun Valley.

1

The big man astride the magnificent black-and-white pinto stallion weaved among gnarled, stunted junipers that grew so thickly he couldn't see over or through them. He had been immersed in this green maze since seven o'clock this morning. But he wasn't lost. A Trailsman doesn't get lost. Temporarily trapped, like now, yes, but never lost. The sun guided him by day, the stars by night, whether he was in the mountains of Colorado, which lay behind him, or the vast semi-arid desert of the New Mexico Territory, which he now rode across.

Occasionally, Skye Fargo glanced at the late October sun to get his bearings. In the absence of any landmarks or a navigator's sextant—which he wouldn't know how to use even if he had one—he had to rely on his dead-reckoning abilities to reach his immediate destination. He estimated Tucson lay approximately 250 miles south by southwest. The vast majority of that distance would be barren desert. The maze of junipers represented a mild annoyance when compared to that cauldron.

Passing through overlapping branches, Fargo came to a wide ravine. He reined the Ovaro to a halt at the edge of it. In the middle of it were shod hoofprints. He counted five sets. One of the horses had thrown its hind left shoe. The Trailsman did not need to dismount and make a closer inspection of the hoofprints to know the riders had headed down the winding ravine at a trot less than two hours ago.

Looking up the draw, Fargo saw where they entered it. He grinned and shook his head. It was obvious to him the riders had run out of patience with bothersome trees, the branches of which clutched and clawed like witches' gnarled fingers, and taken the path of least resistance in the ravine, regardless of where it led.

Fargo chose, however, to proceed along the course he had set. He rode down into the ravine. Crossing the hoofprints, he caught a whiff of smoke and immediately reined to a halt. Had the riders smelled the smoke also, he wondered, and gone to investigate its source? If they had, they were asking for trouble. This was Jicarilla Apache country. Under the very best of conditions, Jicarilla were not the friendly sort.

The Apaches always camped near a source of water. The ravine unquestionably led to a stream. Some of the smoke rising from their cooking fires wafted its way up the meandering draw.

Sitting easy in his saddle, looking down the ravine, Skye Fargo had mixed emotions about what to do; proceed on course, or detour to help the riders get out of a bad fix, if they hadn't already been killed?

He decided to go have a look. If the men had been slain, that would be the end of it. If there were signs of one or more being alive, he would figure out a way to rescue them.

Fargo reined the stallion to follow the hoofprints, then set him to lope. Rounding a soft bend, he saw a thin layer of smoke coming toward him and took to the trees, where he continued to follow the ravine.

After riding a short distance, his wild-creature hearing picked up wailings of the type females make over the loss of a loved one. Frowning, he began to slowly raise his gaze and stopped when he saw black smoke through the juniper's branches. He was close to the Apache campsite. Damn close.

He proceeded with caution and came to a bluff. He eased from his saddle and left the pinto hidden in the junipers while he crawled out on top of the barren bluff to survey things. The ravine did, indeed, lead to water. Torrents of run-offs had carved a deep gully that sliced down the bluff to combine with many other run-offs to create what Fargo knew was a surging, muddy turbulence, now reduced by absorption, then evaporation, to a mere trickle. Another bluff rose well beyond the stream. It was higher than the one on which Fargo lay.

Twelve wickiups stood a short distance above the high-water mark on the near side of the tiny stream. Jicarilla women stood or sat and waited while they watched the temporary shelters burn. Two of the women clutched naked children to their bosoms. Three sat and rocked back and forth. They were covered with the blood of the Jicarilla men whose butchered bodies they clutched. Five females lay faceup, their dead eyes staring at the sun. All five were naked. Even from his lofty perch Fargo's keen vision allowed him to see that their throats had been cut.

He didn't see any ponies or horses, not one live Jicarilla male, nor any of the white men, dead or alive. But he knew they had been there and done this. Warring Indians did not rape and butcher; ruthless, bloodthirsty white men did. The Trailsman had seen these same trappings left by the same kind of no-good white men many times before.

Fargo stood to scan as much of the landscape as he could, mostly up and down the width and length of the barren expanse between the bluffs. He hoped to see the Jicarilla had caught and killed the five men, but he saw only the thin ribbon of water that glistened like silver in the bright sun's rays. Bends at each end of the bluffs, which ran east to west, denied him further eye-search.

Walking to his horse, Fargo reckoned the butchers had

arrived at the encampment at a time when all but three of the Jicarilla men were away on a hunt. The absence of ponies suggested there weren't enough for those three, so they had been left behind to protect the women. In all probability he would find all three to be older men. He mounted up, entered the ravine and followed the shod hoofprints down to the wickiups.

When one of the women spotted him, she alerted the others. They immediately ceased wailing and stood to watch him ride in. Their studious gazes didn't last long, though. They grabbed sticks and stones, then ran to engage the big white man. Fargo fended off the stones, grabbed the fast-moving sticks and yanked them from the women's hands. He broke them in two and flung the pieces away.

Now the enraged females began to try pulling him from the saddle. Fargo did not know one word of the Jicarilla dialect, so he resorted to sign language. He reined the Ovaro to follow a tight circle to keep the women off him while he signed, "I am not here to hurt you. I came to help you."

Although their tempers remained the same, they did back off. Fargo stopped the stallion from circling. He raised both hands to show neither held a weapon, that he came in peace, then signed, "Where are your men?"

The women exchanged nervous glances, then talked it over. Finally, the eldest woman took a step closer to Fargo and signed, "Hunting."

That was what he had thought. He nodded to show he understood her sign, then asked, "How many hunt? In which direction did they go?"

She answered, "Fifteen," then pointed toward the east bend.

He noticed there weren't any young boys around, only girls too young to rape. He believed the boys had gone with the men, a common practice among most other tribes. He inquired, anyhow.

She told him six boys accompanied their fathers.

"Fifteen altogether, or twenty-one?" Fargo signed.

"Twenty-one," she signed back.

Now Fargo knew the strength of the Jicarilla, in case he encountered them. He then asked, "Is there anything I can do to help?" He doubted if there was, but he asked, anyhow.

She told him no. They were going to leave everything as is for the men to see when they returned.

Fargo nodded, then rode among the smoldering wickiups and all around the encampment to find whether or not the three dead men were armed with rifles or carbines, and to spot in which direction the shod hoofprints went when the men left. He saw two broken bows and several arrows, but no guns of any kind. The white butchers had also headed toward the east bend.

He rode back to the women, dismounted and got the sticks of licorice he'd been saving for just such an occasion out of his saddlebags. He twisted them in half and gave a piece to each youngster and woman. They just stared at the black sticks. Fargo had to put a piece in his mouth and start chewing and sucking on it to show them how. He returned to his saddle and headed for the ravine. Looking behind, he saw them standing there, chewing on the licorice, their chins dripping wet with the black juice.

"How strange," Fargo muttered, thoughtfully. What a big difference a little licorice can make, he mused. The settlers going West, the army soldiers, and Washington . . . especially Washington, have been going about it in the wrong way. They should try licorice sticks instead of bullets.

He glanced toward the east bend. Either the Jicarilla had killed the bastards, or they had not. In a way, Fargo hoped they had not. He wanted to punish the dogs. But he knew that was a very remote possibility. They had headed east on clear, level ground. Chances were good he'd never run across them again. If he did, there would be hell to pay. At least they had put the junipers behind, something he still had to suffer a tad longer.

Fargo cleared his mind of all thoughts about the white men and concentrated on putting as much distance between himself and the wickiups as fast as possible. He didn't like the thought of tangling with that many Jicarilla men. When they returned and saw the brutal atrocities committed by the whites, no amount of licorice could bank their fires of hatred. *They will come looking for me to take their revenge out on,* he told himself, *not the butchers, because I'm closer.* Fargo rode up the ravine and left it when he got to the place where he found the shod hoofprints that he now wished he'd never seen. Moments later he was wandering again in the green maze.

An hour before sunset he broke out of the junipers' treeline, which ended on a ridge that overlooked a broad area of flat terrain populated by stone monoliths only. While the view was breathtaking, especially with a lowering sun to lengthen the huge boulders' dark shadows, he refused to tarry and look. Normally, Fargo would, but not now. He remained concerned that the Jicarilla, whom he knew were excellent trackers, were closing in on him. In open country, like that which he viewed from the ridge, they would never catch his powerful stallion. In order to lose the Indians, he would ride until darkness came and swallowed him up. Fargo found a route off the ridge to the enormous stones below.

Passing among the monstrous boulders—several towered unbelievably high—he saw most stood perfectly balanced on single pedestals of smaller stones. He reckoned if he touched one of the brutes it would topple. Millennia of winds and rains, and all they carried, had polished the monoliths and their dainty pedestals as smooth as glass, and wherever the wind and rain had found a soft spot on the great boulders, they sculpted out that soft spot to leave interesting, if not remarkably beautiful, designs. While most were smooth indentations—much like navels—some were tunnel-shaped and went completely through the massive stone.

Fargo's preoccupation with the stately boulders was such that he didn't sense the Jicarilla's presence until it was too late for him to take evasive action. They swarmed from the shadows behind or leapt from atop the sunstruck giant boulders and caught Fargo by surprise. He didn't want to add to their existing misery, but he had no other choice. Twisting and turning the Ovaro, he drew his Colt and shot the nearest three Jicarilla in the leg at point-blank range. Then he dug his heels into the pinto's flanks. The stallion charged out of the forest of stone sentinels.

And ran smack-dab into the young boys. They stood in a line facing him, with their bows and arrows poised to shoot. There was no way the Trailsman would shoot a youngster, even when faced with this life-threatening situation. So he held his fire, took his chances and ploughed through their line. Arrows flew past him going away. He set the Ovaro in a dead-run and rode hellbent for leather to put as much distance between him and the youngsters as he could before any could let another arrow fly.

He looked over his shoulder. Screaming, pony-mounted Jicarilla broke out of great rocks. A dense cloud of dust churned in the ponies' wake. The young boys parted and ran to their ponies. The thundering pack of Indian ponies raced through the gap they left. Fargo looked ahead. He wasn't out of the woods yet.

He reloaded the Colt. Holstering it, he leaned low over the Ovaro's neck and glanced west. The bottom of the huge, fiery red-orange sun appeared to melt and flatten where it touched the horizon. Darkness would come slowly.

An arrow shot past him. Then another. He glanced behind. The leader of the pack and the rider trailing him by half a length were staying up with the Ovaro. They trailed in his dust by about six lengths. Four Jicarilla had given up the chase. The boys lagged far behind. The race continued at a fast pace. Fargo glanced behind occasionally. At twilight it was down to the Ovaro and the two hard-running Indian ponies, and they were sticking with him.

As twilight rapidly faded, giving way to darkness, Fargo came to a rock-strewn area that he couldn't avoid. He wouldn't risk crippling his horse no matter what, and it was getting dark fast. He had two options: halt and shoot them, or proceed with caution. He decided to go with the latter, but keep the other option open. Fargo slowed when he entered the area. Colt in hand, he looked over his shoulder.

The Jicarilla had divided, but not slowed. Fargo knew their strong thirst for vengeance made them take chances. If he were them, he would do the same thing. Ponies could be replaced; an opportunity to kill, like this one, came only once. And that opportunity would soon be lost forever due to darkness. They matched the Ovaro's pace as they rode on his quarters, each no more than ten yards away, with their arrows aimed at him.

Reluctantly, Fargo twisted and shot to wound the man on his right. The bullet hit his upper left arm and knocked him off the pony. Before Fargo could swing around and shoot the fallen man's companion, he heard his bowstring twang.

The arrow plunged into Fargo's back, slightly above the left shoulder blade. His pain was immediate. He fell forward onto the stallion's neck and fired blindly at the bowman.

Concurrent with the third shot he heard the man yelp. He looked in time to see him fall from the pony, then watched him fall to the ground. Fargo hoped he hadn't killed the fellow. Fargo rode on.

Darkness came. Fargo believed he had finally shaken the Jicarilla. He reined the Ovaro to a halt, eased from his saddle, and felt along the arrow's shaft. He knew the point was embedded too deeply to pull it out. But it had to come out, otherwise infection was a certainty.

Gritting his teeth, he reached around and gripped the shaft. When he did, the point moved and searing pain instantly shot outward, all across his back, the left shoulder, the left side of his neck, and down his left arm. Perspiration appeared on his brow. "It's now or never," Fargo grunted. He took a deep breath and shoved.

The brittle shaft broke in two, where it entered his shoulder. Fargo held the fletched end to his face, but he only vaguely saw the feathers, because he was staring blankly into the night, wondering, wondering . . .

Two days later, the area all around the crusted hole in Fargo's back had swelled and become inflamed. He rode on parched earth now, heavily cracked and bone-dry. He thirsted for rain. Oh, how he longed for it. Only rain could soothe the pain that gnawed on his back and shoulder. Only rain could provide his faithful stallion with his fill of water. As the Ovaro relentlessly plodded across the sun-baked earth, his and Fargo's head drooped, and Fargo prayed for rain.

The next day the big man watched through blurred vision dark thunderheads build in the west. It looked as though his prayers were going to be answered.

By mid-afternoon the thunderheads had collected and the air become deathly still. Fargo's lake-blue eyes burned. His chiseled face grew hotter by the moment. His mouth and

17

raspy throat felt parched. His dry, hot lips were cracked. And he heard nothing but the blood in his temporal veins surging in cadence with every heartbeat. It sounded as though sand pumped in them. Fargo realized he was drifting into delirium.

At dusk his delirium was complete. His senses faded in and out. He was burning up with fever. "The arrow," he mumbled incoherently, "must come out." He collapsed forward onto the pinto's neck, his leaden arms hanging down on either side.

Fargo vaguely remembered feeling the cool raindrops on his back, and the Ovaro halting at a pool of muddy water to drink his fill, and him slipping from the saddle and falling alongside the pool. It all happened in slow-motion, as though in a distorted, fuzzy dream, without sound.

The downpour enlarged the pool to the point it spread onto Fargo's face. Coming out of his stupor, he rolled over and pressed up onto hands and knees, touched his lips to the muddy water and swilled. Then he collapsed facedown and rolled out of the water. He lay there with his eyes closed and his brain swimming. Sick and weak, he tried to get up, but could not. His senses began to fade.

Before his hearing left him, Fargo heard men laughing. It sounded as though they were coming toward him, riding in a metal tunnel. He called out of them, and tried to rise again, and failed.

He lay on his side, stared through blurry vision, forgetting all that he heard. Boots broke into his swirling vision. He felt hands shake him, and a whiskey voice that said, "He's alive, but only barely. What do you think, Boss? Kill him, or leave him to die?"

Boss answered, "Get his guns and horse, then leave him for the buzzards."

Numb, sluggish hands tried to prevent them from taking

his Colt, but a boot kicked them away. Fargo vaguely heard the Ovaro knicker a protest, and Boss shout, "Stand still, you purdy son of a bitch! I'm gonna get on you whether you like it or not!"

The last thing Fargo remembered before his mind shut down was hearing the whiskey voice chuckle then say, "Damn, Boss, you let that purdy horse git away."

2

The thunderstorm moved away. In its wake were left fast disappearing puddles and pools of muddy water and a chill in the air. Dawn's early light painted the rain-soaked wasteland in irregular patterns of harsh grays and splotches of black. All was quiet. As the morning sun rose, the sky slowly changed from dull gray to warm colors. When it peeked over the horizon, sunrays kissed still wet saguaro—many thirty or more feet tall—that stood glistening sentinel-like. The Arizona desert slowly awakened.

When the sun was full up, its warmth knocked the chill off the big man laying facedown, half in and half out of the muddy pool. Skye Fargo groaned, stirred partially conscious. His eyes opened slowly, as though it took great effort to lift the eyelids.

For a long moment he lay unmoving, staring at the calm, brown surface of the water, while his confused, feverish brain tried to sort things out and tell him where he was and how he got here.

A fly lit on his left ear and started walking. When he raised his left hand to shoo the fly away, excruciating pain flashed in the shoulder and jarred him fully awake. He relaxed the arm's muscles and the pain subsided. Then he rested a moment, wondered what caused his left shoulder to hurt so much. Had he gone to sleep and fallen off his horse? No. He could feel something heavy in his shoulder. Like a rock.

A big one with jagged edges. Slowly, how it got there came back to him.

He tried to rise to defend himself against the screaming Jicarilla he imagined he heard and saw clutching at him. His gun hand reached for the Colt. When he found the gun missing from its holster, he groped for it under his pillow and felt the grip melt in his hand. He jerked a muddy hand from beneath the pillow and, for the longest, stared in disbelief at it, wondering how the mud got there.

The Ovaro nudged Fargo's rump and emitted a throaty knicker. Fargo came to his knees and tried to bring the stallion into focus, but could not. He had to get away from the angry Jicarilla trying to pull him to the ground between two of the huge boulders. Skye Fargo called upon every ounce of strength that remained in his body to reach up and grab the saddlehorn. Gripping it, he labored to pull himself to stand. He put his left foot in the stirrup and rolled up into the saddle. Fargo fell forward onto the Ovaro's neck.

High fever produced Fargo's delirium, which stayed with him constantly, and affected the working of his inner-clock. Normally it would send a signal to his inert brain and tell it to activate his senses and awaken him, or he would tell it when to shut down and let this body sleep. Delirious, Fargo had no control whatsoever over it. The alarm bell rang and awakened his brain at most any time.

His delirium also affected his brain when it slept or was awake. When it slept, Fargo had nightmarish hallucinations. When it was awake, his senses faded in and out. When they faded in, he would be normal. When they began to fade out, he would start hallucinating.

Fargo's excellent health and strong life-wish kept him in the saddle . . . most of the time. During the next two days, he fell from his saddle seven times, each time for the same reason—a recurring nightmare. He saw himself locked in a death struggle with a faceless Jicarilla Apache man atop one of the extremely tall monoliths. During the struggle, the faceless man always managed to get Fargo's Colt and leave him with no other choice but to jump off the enormous stone. He would see himself falling, tumbling, screaming to a certain death. The Ovaro stood below. Fargo would try to grab his saddlehorn and break the fall, but always missed it. At the last split-second before he hit the onrushing ground, his life-wish kicked in to awaken his brain, his senses would instantly return and the nightmare abruptly end.

He would find himself standing with his gun hand holding onto the saddlehorn, his heart pounding, his body bathed in sweat. Now alert and in full control of his senses, he would rest a moment or two to catch his wind. Then he would give the Ovaro and himself a drink of water from one of his three canteens, munch on beef jerky, mount up, check the sun or constellations to get his bearings, and angle his horse to walk in the correct direction. Eventually, his delirium would return, he would collapse onto the stallion's neck, and the whole process would repeat itself.

Time took its toll on what little strength Fargo still had, and his brain slept far more than it was awake.

Burning up with fever, and terribly weak, Fargo was totally unaware of the violent standstorm that consumed him and the Ovaro. Therefore, when the stallion halted at a circular, stone-rimmed water well, Fargo did not know it. But the instant hands touched him, the nightmare manifested and he resisted. Nonetheless, he saw himself falling awkwardly. Like always, just before he hit the ground, he awakened, but this time it was different. He found himself not holding onto the saddlehorn, but lying facedown on a bed, staring at the tiny flame of a short, fat candle. Then Fargo saw, in the dim light cast by and behind the flame, Jesus nailed to his cross, and brought him into focus. Hanging there with his chin on his chest, Jesus seemed to be looking at his blood that leaked from the wound inflicted by the Roman soldier's spear.

His gaze was interrupted and he looked away when he heard a man say in Spanish, "Maria, wet a cloth and bring it to me. Hurry, daughter."

He heard water slosh, then felt the wet cloth gently move all around and over his shoulder wound.

A female voice spoke in a low, concerned tone: "That's ugly looking, Papa. It's infected. What do you suppose caused it?"

"An arrow," Fargo mumbled.

An old man's face appeared before Fargo's half-closed eyes. "Eh, *senor*? What did you say?"

Fargo's senses were fading out fast. Whispering softly, he repeated the two words.

The old man frowned, put an ear close to Fargo's mouth and asked him to say them again.

Fargo strained to speak louder and barely whispered, "An arrowhead is . . ." As the unfinished sentence trailed off, the tiny flame disappeared, and Jesus vanished. Fargo closed his eyes, and his brain went back to sleep.

Distorted hallucinations started almost immediately. He saw himself laying facedown beside a bubbling pool of brimstone in the fires of hell. The Ovaro watched Mary help Jesus get off the cross, then both came and knelt by him. Jesus used the Roman's spear to slice across Fargo's wound. Oddly, Fargo felt no pain. Mary put her slender right foot on one edge of the cut and her hands on the other, then pulled it open for Jesus. Fargo screamed when Jesus reached in the wound and pulled out a festered black glob of foul-smelling raw tissue that grew in size, then changed into Satan, who started struggling with Jesus. The nightmare faded away before Fargo saw who won, good or evil.

Twice two pretty *senoritas*, Maria and Tia, came close to bringing him all the way out of his stupor by drenching him with ice-cold water. His brain tried to awaken his senses, but they came to him only partway then sped away. He saw, heard, felt, smelled, and tasted in flashes. The Ovaro looked on from where he stood in heavy shadows. Jesus watched from where he hung on his cross. In both instances, after dousing him, the *senoritas* looked at the hurt spot on the back of his shoulder, commented that it looked better, then kissed his lips.

Fargo's fever broke during the night on the second day. All his senses simply switched on and functioned normally. He felt weak, of course, weak as all hell, when he sat up in the bed. Some pain, light and tolerable, tugged in his wound when he moved his shoulder forward to see it in the glow cast by the tiny flame. When he could not glimpse the wound, he felt over it with the middle finger on his right hand. A vertical streak of narrow crust bisected a large patch of it where the arrow entered. The swelling around it had gone down slightly since the last time he remembered touching it. The swelling was warm to his touch. He didn't feel the point embedded in his flesh, and wondered who got it out.

He wondered about a lot of things, mostly about missing pieces to a puzzle that would tell how he came to be sitting naked in this bed in a candlelit bedroom that smelled of hay. Fargo searched his memory for the missing pieces, but all he found were fragments. He remembered where he was going when the Jicarilla put the arrow in his back, and started his recollections from the time of that unfortunate incident and came forward.

"I broke the damn arrow off too close to shove it on through," he muttered under his breath. "I rode with the point in me . . . how long before the delirium set in? Two, three days?'' Fargo couldn't remember. An *olla* filled with water stood on the earthen floor next to the bed. He dipped a cupped hand into it. As he drank a handful of the cool water, it prompted another remembrance. He recalled falling off his horse. ''Yes, it happened during a rainstorm at night. I fell into a puddle of water. Men laughed at me. They stole my stallion. One of the men called another 'Boss.' Boss spoke in a whiskied voice. Boss stole my pinto. Then how did I get here? Walk?''

The Ovaro knickered. Fargo jerked his head around to face the throaty sound. He became confused when he saw his stallion. The pinto stood munching hay in dark shadows at the back part of what Fargo now recognized as being not a bedroom, but a large, enclosed shed.

He quit trying to fit the pieces of the memory puzzle together, laid on his good side and told himself that whoever removed the point would come back to check on him. At that time, he would have the person to fill in the blanks. Fargo drifted into sleep staring at the small, pedestal-mounted icon of Jesus hanging on the cross that stood behind the fat candle on a little wooden box.

The instant hinges squeaked, his eyes snapped open. His gun hand automatically reached under the pillow to grasp the big Colt's handle. Alarmed, his eyes widened when he didn't find it. He then drew his left shin up to withdraw the Arkansas-toothpick from its calf-sheath, but neither it nor the stiletto were there. He balled his gun hand beneath the pillow, narrowed his eyes to mere slits, and peered through the scant openings while he listened and waited for the intruder to approach within striking reach.

A door grated open. Fargo heard muted footsteps come toward the bed, felt his sheet leave his back. A man grunted the Spanish words, "*Muy bueno,*" then lowered the sheet. Fargo relaxed, opened his fist and eyes, and turned to look at the man.

"Oho, *senor,* I see you are awake!" the old man chortled in Spanish before he caught himself and shifted to English. He stepped around the bed and sat next to the wooden box so he would be at eye-level with the big Anglo stranger. "Are you well? Are you hungry?" As he said it, the old man winced, then bitterly chastised himself, "Stupid old man, of course he's hungry!" He gestured an apology, then said, "My daughter is making breakfast while I looked at your sore place. You are too feeble to walk to the house." Rising he added, "I will bring the food to you, *senor.*"

Fargo liked him at once, not because of the offer of food and not because he offered to bring it, but because he was gentle.

The old man—Fargo guessed his age at between sixty-five and seventy—had a mane of silver, unruly hair, stood about five feet tall, and carried no more than ninety pounds of weight. Clear dark-brown eyes twinkled mischievously from either side of his shiny, broad-tipped, light-brown nose. A wide mouth with full lips a shade browner than his complexion dominated his facial features. He wore a dingy-white tilma-like garment and walked barefooted. A tiny silver medallion hung at the bottom of a tightly braided strand of red horsetail hairs looped around his slim neck. Fargo believed the relief on the medallion would be of the old man's patron saint.

Fargo said in Spanish, "No, stay for a moment or two longer. I need to ask—"

Turning back, the old man interrupted to say, "Eh? *Senor* speaks my language?"

Fargo answered, "A little. I'm rusty, though. I rarely get the opportunity to hear and speak it. What do I call you?"

The old man shrugged as he replied, "Pedro. Pedro

Fuentes. Or Papa. That's what the people in our little village call me. Papa.''

"Is the medallion you wear around your neck of Saint Peter?''

Papa raised and kissed it, then answered, "No, *senor*. Saint Latro. A very old and most gentle priest gave it to me. I had done a bad thing. He told me that when he was young that he, too, did bad things. A priest from Greece gave him the medallion, and he gave it to me.''

"Do you mind telling me what you did that was so bad it moved an old priest to pass the medallion on to you? You don't seem to have an evil bone in your body.''

"We don't think about it, but when I was a young man I killed a man for bothering my mother. She was a widow, you see, and had nobody else to protect her from Feo's advances. So I cut Feo's throat, God forgive me.'' He quickly crossed himself.

Fargo wondered if God would forgive him for killing all the men he'd had to. He'd never shot or stabbed to death an unarmed man. He'd used his hands to kill unarmed men out to kill him. And he'd never killed an armed one, unless the man pulled iron and threw down on him first, or unless he came at him gripping a knife. In some way the other man had to start it, for Fargo to send him to Boot Hill. Fargo wondered if that made any difference to God when He kept score in his Black Book. "Where am I?'' he asked. "Arizona Territory?''

"*Si, senor*. Our village has no official name. We call it *villa deserto del diablo*. Where are you going?''

"Tucson.''

Pedro nodded. "*Si*, I can walk to Tucson in less than fifteen days, God willing.''

Fargo reckoned he was about two, maybe three days from his destination. Feeling tired suddenly, Fargo released Pedro and told him, "We will talk more later, after we have Maria's breakfast." When he spoke the name, he wondered how he knew it.

Pedro did, too. The mischievous twinkle in his eyes changed into one of concern as he inquired, "How do you know my daughter's name? Has Maria been bothering you? If she has, I'll whip her."

Fargo managed a chuckle. "No whipping necessary, Papa. Just a lucky guess on my part. You can go now. Please, leave the door open."

Again, Pedro nodded. Barely, this time. He acted as though he was uncertain about his daughter's morals, and in a oblique way questioned them when he asked, "Are you sure?"

"Yes, I'm sure," Fargo answered, although he now questioned them also. Papa knew his daughter's morals a damn sight better than he. If Maria had "bothered" him, he didn't know it.

He watched Pedro hurry out and go to the back door of an adobe hovel that stood about twenty yards away. Similar adobe abodes were on both sides of Pedro's. Less than a foot separated them. More often than not, the hovels joined; the two homes shared a common wall. Fargo had been in these kind of villages before. He knew there was much more to this one than he could see through the open doorway. The path connecting the two structures looked more like a much-used groove than anything else.

When Pedro stepped into his home, Fargo rolled onto his back—the pain could go to hell; Fargo hadn't knowingly been in a bed in a month of Sundays. It felt good. Sighing, he closed his eyes.

Fargo didn't go to sleep, though. He wanted to, but a one-sided shouting contest erupted inside Pedro's hovel. Eyes closed, Fargo lay there and listened.

Throughout the village dogs started to bark or howl. Fargo answered with a howl of his own. He worked up to it, beginning with a tough-sounding growl, that led into what he thought was a mean snarl, that changed into a series of pitiful barks—as though the shouting made the dog's head ache—and ended with two long, drawn-out howls similar to coyotes howling at the moon—which Fargo had heard many times. He thought he copied them darn good.

Almost immediately, something rough and wet nudged his left hand. His eyes instantly popped open. He saw he had called up a big, solid yellow bitch and her little of young puppies. The excited, playful puppies crawled into bed with him. Tails wagging, they romped, practiced growling as they chewed on his arms and legs, wrestled with his sheet and pillow, licked his face. The bitch lay and watched.

Fargo corraled them all—he counted six—in his hands and arms and told them to hush and listen. Their limber ears tried to raise, as though they were obeying him, but the puppies' attention span didn't last long. All but one—the runt of the litter—scampered off the bed and scattered in search of something else to terrorize.

He put the runt on his chest, rubbed her face and ears while he went back to listening to Maria give Papa a razor-sharp tongue lashing. Words spewed out of her mouth in a steady stream, not unlike Fargo emptying the Colt of bullets in rapid fire, and just as blistering hot. He caught enough of the monologue to know Papa had accused her of "bothering" the wounded Anglo in the shed.

The tempo of her scorching verbal assault accelerated. Maria added screams to her shouts as she berated the poor man. Fargo imagined him calmly sitting in a chair, eyes and mouth closed, nodding at all the right times—a study in self-control—and a tubby woman half again his size and double his weight, shaking her fists in his face. Fargo heard pots and pans start clattering, then glass breaking, and knew Maria was slinging things against a wall, all the while vocally denying, denying, denying his accusation.

He turned over on his stomach and repositioned the runt and himself so he could watch the back door. A pan sailed through it and bounced crazily when it came to ground. Then a spindly little girl—he guessed she hadn't seen her twelfth birthday—came out looking over her shoulder. Pedro hadn't mentioned having two daughters. The young girl hurried so fast on the footpath that she tripped over herself twice. As she ran into the shed, Fargo rolled onto his back and laid the puppy on his chest.

The girl came to the bed and looked down at him. Fargo saw she wasn't a young girl at all, but a full-grown, albeit petite, woman who resembled one. He reckoned her age at twenty-five.

Maria had a face that belonged on a pretty doll. Jet-black hair hung to her shapely hips. She wore a white cotton sheath-type dress having no belt or buttons. She had pulled the collar down on her arms just below the shoulders and kept it in place with a drawstring in the collar. The hem fell to her ankles. The thin material left nothing it covered to Fargo's imagination. She had small breasts, the proud nipples of which made twin peaks in the flimsy material.

She stood with her bare feet parted, hands on hips, her flared coal-black eyes flashing angrily. Mad as all hell, she trembled when she spat, "Did you tell Papa I screwed you? Eh? Did you?"

"No. Did you?"

"No!" she yelled, and the runt emitted a frightened yap.

"If you say so," Fargo toyed. "I was out like that candle's flame, so I wouldn't have known."

Exasperated, she sighed, cocked her head and looked at the rafters. Her fury abating somewhat, she asked the rafters,

"Why does Papa accuse me of doing bad things?" She moved her gaze back to Fargo. In a calm, lower tone of voice, Maria said, "Nothing, absolutely nothing happened. Believe me, nothing at all." She glanced at and nodded toward his wounded shoulder, and inquired, "Does it hurt bad?"

"A little. Not much. Did you doctor me?"

"I helped. You don't remember anything? Nothing?"

Fargo shook his head. "No, not really. I drifted in and out. Out mostly."

She sat on the edge of the bed and looked into his eyes for a long moment, all her hostility now put aside. Finally she spoke: "*El diablo* made a terrible sandstorm. It lasted two days and nights. Nobody could go out in it. Papa said he thought he heard a horse knicker. I told him he heard *el diablo*. Papa went to the door and looked outside, anyhow."

"And what did Papa see?"

"Your pretty horse stood at the village well. You were slumped over his neck, ready to fall. Your arms hung down. Standing, looking out the door, we believed you were dead, that *el diablo* had killed you."

"But I wasn't. Please, go on."

"So Papa and I, we went out to see if you were really dead. When he moved your head to check your eyes, you groaned. Papa keeps this old bed out here in the burro's shed so he can take a nap on it during the day. He suggested we carry you to it."

When Maria paused, Fargo said, "You two and my stallion saved my life. For that, I am truly eternally grateful. Bring my saddlebags to me, please."

He propped on one elbow to watch her go to the back of the shed. His saddle and bedroll sat on a pile of hay near his horse. Tied to upright frames of slim poles were several sticks that held the old man's implements—pitchfork, shovel, coiled wire and the like—and draped on one were the saddlebags that she brought to him.

Fargo opened one flap and removed a pair of two-inch-long silver earrings he had been saving for just such an occasion. He handed them to Maria, saying, "These are but a small token of my appreciation for your great deed."

Maria smiled hugely. Tears welled in her eyes as she looked at them. She put them on, pushing her long hair back and asked, "How do they look on me? Pretty good, eh?"

They did look good on her, and he told her so.

She moved the puppy away to make room for herself, then fell forward onto his muscled chest and kissed him. Her hot tongue found his and sucked on it. Fargo became aroused immediately. The sheet over his groin started rising. One of her hands slipped under the sheet and slid down over his abdomen, through his pubic hair and curled around the base of his hardening member.

Maria broke the kiss. Gazing into his eyes, she whispered, "We might as well. I've already been accused." She squeezed gently but firmly.

Before he could answer, a chorus of childish giggles came from the front of the shed. Fargo's hard-on limbered and wilted in Maria's grasp. Both of them looked toward the open door.

A small crowd of village children—toddlers to preteen-agers—vied for a look inside. Several stood with curious eyes at gaps between the adobe bricks in the front wall. An older girl among those in the doorway made a shamey-shame gesture. In a lilting voice she said, "Na-na-nee-na, Maria's being bad, again, Maria's being bad, again, na-na-nee-na."

Maria came off the bed and ran toward the girl. Motioning for all of them to leave, she shouted, "*Vayan de aqui!* And don't come back! He doesn't want to be bothered by you!"

The kids scattered and fled, shrieking and giggling, in all directions. Maria lingered in the doorway to make sure they left. Fargo saw Pedro crane out the back door, apparently to see what caused the commotion. Finally he stepped outside and faced Maria.

She told him, "Go back inside, Papa. No one's hurt. Carmensita and her little brothers and sisters were pestering us. I chased them away."

In a way, Fargo felt thankful to see Pedro head for the shed. Fargo was really still too weak to romp with Maria, even though he would have damn sure tried if not for the interruption.

Coming into the shed, Pedro was all smiles. "Daughter, go prepare another breakfast for *mi amigo,* while he and I finish talking." Pedro glanced at Fargo and added, *"Eh, amigo?"*

"Look at my pretty earrings, Papa." Maria drew her hair back so he could see them.

Pedro gave them a passing glance. "They are nice. Now, *andole,* daughter, and do what I told you."

She flashed a smile to Fargo, then left.

Pedro hunkered next to the bed. "You gave the pretty earrings to her, eh?"

Fargo nodded. He didn't want to discuss the earrings. Fargo needed some answers. "Where are my Colt and Sharps?"

"Eh?" The old man's eyes cut to the pinto.

It occurred to Fargo that Pedro didn't know the weapons by their proper names. "My pistol and rifle."

Pedro shook his head. *"Senor,* you had no guns when I pulled you from the saddle. I would have seen them if you had."

Fargo reached in a dark corner of his memory bank to

search for the answer. Slowly a word picture emerged. Absentmindedly, Fargo muttered, "Boss tried to steal my horse."

"Eh? Who?"

"Boss. Boss took my guns. I'm sure he did. Son of a bitch! I'm naked without my weapons." He looked at Pedro's puzzled expression and asked, "My stiletto. Where is it?"

"Stiletto? No *comprendo, senor.*"

"Knife."

The old man's eyes brightened. "Oh, knife? *Si, senor,* you had a knife. Maria found it on your leg when she removed your boots and pants. The knife and scabbard are in the house. I wiped all the blood off of it. It is clean and shiny now."

Fargo frowned. He didn't recall leaving any blood on the stiletto the last time he cleaned it. And he hadn't used it since. *Or have I?* he wondered. He double-checked the old man. "The knife had blood on it?"

Pedro nodded, said, *"Si, senor.* Your blood. I used the knife—I must say it is a very sharp knife—to cut your wound open. Maria held it open while I dug around in the flesh to get the arrowhead out. I kept the arrowhead so I could show it to you when you got better. It's in the house. I'll go get it."

Fargo watched him rise and head for the house. On the way, he passed Maria bringing the breakfast and a coffeepot. As she entered the shed and came toward the bed, Fargo smelled the aromas of Mexican food and coffee.

Maria put the coffeepot on the ground within easy reach for him and the plate next to the candle on the box. Handing him a fork and cup, she asked, "Feel like sitting? Or do you want me to feed you? Eh?"

Never had coffee smelled so good to him. He needed some in the worst way. Fargo sat and held his cup out to her.

Filling it, she asked, "What did you and Papa talk about? My bothering you? Eh?"

Eyes closed, Fargo brought the cup to his lips but did not part them to sip yet. First he inhaled slowly, deeply of the steaming brew until his lungs filled with its aroma, then held the breath. Releasing the breath slowly, he opened his eyes partway and grinned. He threw the grin in not because of what she asked, but because it felt so damn good to be alive and to be having coffee. After taking a sip, he told her what they talked about.

Maria sat handy to the coffeepot and watched him eat the four eggs she had scrambled with chiles and onions. He folded some in a corn tortilla which he used to help scoop the rest on his fork, bite by bite. Hungry as a she-wolf with pups, he quickly downed his meal.

Fargo wiped the plate clean with the last bite of folded tortilla, then poked it in his mouth and held his cup for her to refill.

Pedro walked up as Maria tilted the coffeepot to pour. In his hands were the Arkansas-toothpick, its calf-sheath, and the arrowhead. Taking the stiletto, Fargo washed down his mouthful of food. He gave the blade a cursory glance, not that he needed to—he trusted the old man's word—but because Pedro looked on and obviously sought Fargo's approval. Laying the knife on the bed, Fargo said, "You did a good job, Papa. Clean as a hound's tooth. Thanks."

When he gestured for the sheath and point, Pedro handed them to him. Fargo laid the sheath aside to inspect the point. "How did something this small feel as heavy as a big rock in me?" he mused aloud. The flint point, he saw, was quite sharp on its serrated edges but noticeably blunt on the tip— the reason why it had not gone all the way through his shoulder. He mentally censured the Jicarilla for not paying closer attention to his craftsmanship. "Sloppy work," he muttererd. Setting the arrowhead on his pillow, Fargo inquired about his clothes.

Maria said they were so muddy she had to scrub them twice. "I cleaned your boots and hat, belt and gun belt, too. Everything is clean. They are on my bed. I'll go get them. Eh?" She picked up the plate and left.

While she was gone, Fargo drank coffee, and he and Pedro chatted. Pedro asked why he was going to Tucson and where he came from. "I'm going to Tucson to visit a friend I met in Fort Worth, Texas, a couple of years back. I heard Abel Poteet is the town's sheriff. But the wilderness is my home. I'm very comfortable living in the forests and mountains." He paused when he saw a vacant stare appear in the old man's eyes, then asked, "You don't know what I'm talking about, do you, Papa?"

Pedro shook his head.

The Trailsman described the wilderness to him. As he was doing so, Maria returned, her arms laden with his neatly folded clothes and leather goods. She knelt beside her old father, and they both listened with faraway looks in their eyes, completely captivated by Fargo's vivid descriptions of green mountain forests, beautiful valleys filled with wildflowers, gurgling streams and cascading waterfalls; it went on and on.

When he finished, Maria murmured, "That was so beautiful, so clear in my mind that I saw it. Papa, have you ever seen mountains like those, tall trees and waterfalls? Eh, Papa?"

Pedro shook his head. "No. All I have seen is the devil's desert. A long time ago, I heard about such places and things. But those who told me about them did not make me see any of it like he did. *Como tu llamo, amigo?*"

"Skye. Skye Fargo."

"That is a very pretty name," Maria intoned through a sigh.

Fargo pulled his underwear on, then withdrew the sheet covering his lower torso and worked his Levi's up to his muscled thighs. When he stood to finish pulling them up, purple-white stars swirled in his brain. He collapsed awkwardly across the bed and closed his eyes until the dizzy spell went away.

Concerned, Pedro asked, "Are you all right, *senor*?"

"Here, let me help you stand and put your clothes on," Maria suggested. She held out both hands for him to take.

Fargo held them tightly as she heaved and he came up into a sitting position. Straddling his shins to pull on his socks and boots, Maria assured, "I will have you walking in no time." She grunted while tugging on his boots.

Fargo wondered if they were that difficult to get on his feet, or if the grunts were caused by her crotch rubbing on his hard shinbones. Finally, they were on. He stood and grabbed hold of her shoulders to brace himself.

Pedro dropped Fargo's buckskin shirt over the big man's head. He let go of Maria's shoulders, found he could stand rocksteady, and worked the shirt down his body. Maria buttoned his fly, sneaked a feel, then fed his belt through the loops. Fargo bucked it, then slipped the gun belt around his hips and buckled it. He looked at the empty holster and shook his bowed head. He asked Pedro if he had a gun to sell.

"No, *senor,* I don't have a gun. There are no guns in *villa deserto del diablo.* We are poor peons, *senor.* Too poor to buy bullets to shoot in them if we had any. What little money we have goes for seeds and tools."

Fargo nodded. "Show me your little village," he said, and walked toward the door.

Pedro and Maria fell in alongside him, prepared to steady him should he wobble. But their help wasn't necessary. The more he walked, the more confidence Fargo got. By the time they reached the low adobe wall that boxed around the village, Fargo ambled along like he did before the Jicarilla wounded him. Inside the walls were the villagers' meager crops, now dry stalks.

Pedro told him they grew corn and beans mostly, and, of course, green and red chiles. Twice a year a group of men took the village carts to Phoenix to work in the fields there to earn the money to buy hay. He went on to explain the men were in Phoenix now and that was the reason for so little hay in the shed, and why Fargo saw no carts or burros.

The people either came out to watch the trio or stood in their doorways. The big yellow bitch and her playful puppies followed close behind Fargo. Other dogs lay in shade to watch. Chickens and guinea hens and one peacock roamed at will, as did a sizeable goat herd. Maria explained that no one person or family owned the goats and fowls, they belonged to the village.

The village, Fargo noted, was comprised of four corridors barely wide enough to allow carts passage. Connected hovels having flat roofs lined both sides of the corridors, which came together in the middle of the village and formed a large, circular intersection in the center of which stood the community well, where the Ovaro had stopped. Pedro and Maria's abode stood on the northeast corner of the passageway that ran north from the great circle. *Villa deserto del diablo* had no mission.

They returned to the shed shortly after high noon. Maria left to prepare a midday meal. Pedro said he was tired and thought he would go in and have an early *siesta*. He left. Fargo went to his stallion and checked his hooves and shoes for condition and security. If Fargo felt as good in the morning as he did now, he figured he would head out for Tucson. He dug the dandy brush out of the saddlebags and put it to work cleaning the Ovaro's coat. By the time Maria appeared with two plates of Spanish rice, pinto beans, corn, and *cabrito* he had the coat gleaming.

They sat in a ribbon of shade outside the shed to eat, because Fargo said he wanted to look at something other than four walls. Maria finished eating first. Offering scraps of *cabrito* to the runt, she asked, "Can I bother you now? Eh, Skye?"

As he scanned the backs of the hovels, he muttered, "Someone might barge in on us. I don't like being interrupted, and I'm not an exhibitionist."

She chuckled.

"What's so funny?"

"You. There is no one to barge in on us. We are the only two who are not taking *siesta*. It's safe. Eh, Skye?"

"Then why do I see Carmensita standing at a window, peering out at us?"

Maria's flared eyes cut to the window. Carmensita ducked, but not in time to escape being seen by her.

Fargo suggested, "We wait for night, then you can come bother me all you want, for as long as you want." He set his plate on the ground near the puppy. "That's a promise."

Scraping his and her plates of scraps on the ground for the puppy, she sighed heavily, glanced at the window and said in a disgusted tone of voice, "I see I need to have a serious talk with Carmen on the subject of bothering. Maybe your suggestion is best. I will go take my *siesta* and get *mucho* rest so I can bother you all night. Eh, Skye?"

"That would be wise."

Maria got up and went to the house. Fargo watched her buttock cheeks fighting to get out of the dress.

He sat a while longer, then took a turn around the village again. Fargo was restless, and he didn't know why. He walked to the west wall, leaned on it and stared across the desert. His was one of those kind of stares that saw everything and nothing, because he didn't bring anything into focus. He went to the well and looked down it, then sat on its edge and glanced down the four corridors. He didn't see any of the fowls or goats. "They, too, are taking *siestas,*" he muttered. Several dogs, including big yaller and her litter, lay on the shady side of what Fargo called South Street. Naming them was something to do. Finally, he drifted back to the shed.

He went to his horse and looked at his hooves and shoes again. Gazing through the doorway, he decided to take the stallion outside. "You want some fresh air? Eh, boy?" he asked the horse.

He rode bareback and without reins. What started out to be walking exercise soon changed into running him outside the walls. Coming back he took the pinto over the north wall. Satisfied that the Ovaro was as fit as a fine tuned fiddle, and that he could stay on him, Fargo dismounted and led him through the opening in the north wall. Scratching the stallion's face, he told him, "Go run and play in the sand, boy." The Ovaro didn't move. Fargo had to slap his rump to get him going. The pinto took off running, snorting, throwing his head wildly. Fargo watched him for a long moment, then glanced at the lowering sun. He reckoned it hung at about four o'clock. He ambled back to the bed, sat to pull off his boots, then lay back and pulled his hat down over his eyes. He felt the runt crawl in and snuggle up to him. Soon, both were sound asleep.

The runt growled softly. Fargo awakened instantly but kept his eyes closed. He heard footsteps approaching his bed. When he felt the runt's tail wagging, he knew Maria was near. His hat came away from his face. He opened his eyes and saw two things; night had fallen, and Maria had taken off her dress.

She didn't say anything as she went about undressing him. Neither did she speak when she entered the bed.

He felt one of her hands grip his member and squeeze and pull. They lay there until she had brought him up rock-hard. When he moved to roll her onto her back, she resisted, and suggested, "No, Skye, let me be on top. You can lay there and rest while I do all the work."

He eased back and let her have her way. She straddled him, then gripped his staff and touched its head to her lower charm and parted those lips with it. Fargo felt the moist warmth as she inserted his crown. She took her hand away, squatted hard and he went in deeply.

She whimpered, "Oh, oh, so big, so big. My belly's full." Then she attacked. She writhed and wiggled, swayed her hips and pumped, all the while lolling her head and tossing it. One second her long hair covered Fargo's face, and the next it dragged over his chest.

She fell forward and rode high as she fed her left nipple between Fargo's lips. As he sucked in almost all of the supple breast, she begged, "Harder. Suck it harder, Skye. Bite me, too. Oh, please bite it."

His hands grasped her buttock cheeks and pulled. She got the idea and bore down every time his hips raised. The opening to her hot tunnel fused around his base and, locked firmly together, they moved in unison, she circling clockwise, him counter-clockwise. She started whimpering again, "Oh, oh, that feels so good, so wonderful. Don't stop, please don't."

Fargo couldn't hold back any longer. She murmured, "Let it go, oh, yes, let it go."

Dogs started to bark. Fargo became attentive. Maria told him they were always barking at night. "Probably at a snake," she whispered. "I'm not through. I'll let you rest a minute or two, and then—"

"Be quiet and listen," he interrupted. Fargo thought he heard horses pounding in.

"I don't hear anything," she muttered.

He felt certain he heard hoofbeats. The Ovaro? He glanced to the back of the shed. His horse wasn't there. He relaxed. She laid on her left side and put her right arm over his chest. The dogs continued to bark. They were running to the north wall. Fargo felt positive he was hearing more than one horse coming. He got up and went to the door. Maria hugged him from behind, pleading, "Come back to bed, darling. It's nothing."

No sooner said than when they both heard the horses jump the north wall and the riders laugh. Fargo asked, "Where is my stiletto?"

"Papa took it back to the house. You want—"

This time gunfire interrupted her. A dog yelped painfully. People darted outside and looked around, but they didn't last long. There was more gunfire as the riders rode down North Street to the well. Women started screaming.

Fargo pulled Maria out of the doorway and warned, "It's best we stay in the shed. I think I know who they are. If I'm correct, they are bloodthirsty devils." Fargo hungered for his weapons. He'd kill the rotten bastards and feel no remorse. But he didn't have his guns. Boss had them. And that meant Fargo was reduced to cowering buck naked in the shed.

Maria cried, "I must hurry to Papa! He's too old to fight them off!"

As she uttered the words, they heard Papa's scream and the gunshot that cut it short. Two tall men ran outside and looked directly at Fargo. They had him cornered. To leave the shed would be suicidal. They would gun him down for sure. Fargo withdrew from the doorway, hoping the butchers had not spotted him. Backing away, he felt something solid bash his head, then the inside of his skull went black.

He came to slowly and confused. Hay covered him. His head and face were bloody. He vaguely heard Maria scuffling with someone, and her frightened voice plead, "Please, please don't hurt me." Then her scream was clipped as Papa's had been, but there was no gunshot to silence her.

Woozy beyond belief, Fargo threw the hay off him and started to rise. The muzzle flash of a revolver briefly lit up the interior of the shed.

The impact of the bullet knocked Skye Fargo back down on the hay. For the second time this night, everything went black.

3

Fargo's senses gradually returned. He heard men talking. At first, it sounded as though they spoke from deep within a cave, and he stood outside at the mouth and listened. He knew they were talking, but they were too far away for him to make out the words.

His nostrils discerned a pronounced sweet odor at first. Then, through the sweetness came the smells unique to horses and their dung.

Fargo's eyes opened slowly. At first they saw only darkness, then, ever so slowly light filtered through it, but in an eerie sort of way, ghostly, as though diffused by a dense fog. Three shadowy, indistinct forms stood over him. He brought them into focus. Gray tones manifested and gave the forms defined shapes. He saw three men, one shorter than the other two. They were speaking Spanish in low tones, as one might when looking down on a corpse lying in a coffin.

He felt the warmth of bedding under him, the coolness of a sheet on his body. Dull pain clogged his left shoulder, left it feeling enlarged and unusually heavy.

Fargo groaned.

The men hushed.

The shorter one stepped closer, bent over and looked at Fargo's eyes. "Can you see and hear me, *senor*?"

Fargo mumbled, "Yes. Where am I?" His head ached.

He felt over it, and found a small gash, his hair matted from the blood that had also trickled to his left ear and down that side of his neck.

"Papa Fuente's shed. You don't remember what happened? The Anglos shooting you?"

Fargo touched his left shoulder. He knew at once the sticky liquid his fingers felt was blood. His fingers searched for the wound and found it high on the shoulder.

The short man went on to say, "Ramon and Jorge found you when they returned from Phoenix and brought in the hay."

The fog in Fargo's brain lifted. Now he remembered everything. He sat up, looking around. Dawn's early light spilled through the open doorway, crept through cracks in the adobe bricks. An empty two-wheel wagon stood outside the door. Four burros stood with the Ovaro, eating hay at the back of the shed. An overturned *olla* lay on the ground about where he was when backing away from the door and feeling the hard blow that knocked him out. The runt's lifeless body lay belly-up near the pile of hay where he had been shot. "Maria?" he asked.

All three men crossed themselves. The short man, obviously their spokesman, answered matter of factly, "Dead. The Anglos cut her throat. It was a horrible thing they did to Maria.

Fargo closed his eyes and shuddered. He had been correct. The maniacal butchers had come to *villa deserto del diablo* to spill blood, rape, and plunder. He knew the short man's answer before he asked the question. "And Papa?"

"Papa is dead, *senor*. Those who did not run into the desert died horrible deaths at the hands of the Anglos. Eleven men, women, and children died."

"How many Anglos were there?"

"Five, *senor*."

"Did anyone hear them say names?"

The short fellow shook his head. "You must leave our village, *senor.*"

Fargo had every intention of doing just that. But the way it was put to him sounded more like a command than a suggestion. The short one was being—"What is your name, *senor*?" Fargo asked.

"Chico. Do not make trouble for us, *senor.* I insist that you leave."

Fargo hadn't missed the sudden change in the tenor of Chico's words. Clearly, Chico was ordering him to go, the implication being if he did not, then Ramon and Jorge and others like them would hound him till he did. Chico mirrored the sentiments of all the villagers. *They are scared to death the butchers will return to make sure my body is among the dead.* Fargo nodded.

Chico stepped back and joined Ramon and Jorge to wait and watch. Fargo tore the sheet into six-inch wide strips and used one to wipe blood off his chest and back. That from the gash had dried. He would take care of it later. While cleaning up he found the hole where the bullet came out high on the back of his left shoulder, above and slightly closer to his neck than the previous wound. He asked Chico to bandage the new wound, but Chico refused. One of the taller men came and took the strips from Fargo.

While he made two compresses, Fargo asked, "What is your *nombre, amigo*?"

"Jorge," he muttered.

"Bind me tight, Jorge. I have a long ride ahead of me. If it comes loose, I won't be able to fix it. *Comprendo*?"

Jorge nodded.

"Will you and Ramon saddle my horse for me?"

"*Si, senor.*" He turned and asked Ramon to saddle the Anglo's horse.

While Ramon complied, Jorge bound the compresses tightly, then stepped back and watched Fargo dress. Although weakened from loss of blood—and the shoulder now hurt like hell's fires—Fargo gritted his teeth and willed himself to ignore all of it. He was determined to ride out of the village, sitting tall in the saddle.

Dressed, Fargo stepped to the Ovaro and secured his bedroll and saddlebags behind the saddle. As he did, he cut his eyes to the saddlecase. The emptiness of it triggered a flash of fury that raged within his body, then collected in his soul. If not for Boss taking my guns, he told himself, none of this would have happened. I will hunt the bastard butchers down, he vowed. When I find them they will die. All five. He quit thinking about it and led his stallion outside.

The morning sun was inches away from making its appearance. Walking to the hovel to get his stiletto and its calf-sheath, Fargo neither saw nor heard anyone, not even one chicken, goat, nor dog.

Inside, he passed through the kitchen and noticed everything was spic and span clean. He saw two other rooms connected by two open archways. He stepped from the kitchen into what was obviously Maria's bedroom. A little doll set propped on her pillow, the icon of the crucifix stood between two unlighted tapers on a shelf. He went into Papa's room. He saw the old man had met his maker on his blood-soaked bed. He retrieved the stiletto and its sheath from a shelf across the room from the death bed. When he picked them up he saw the arrowhead. He put it in a front pocket, then sat in a rickety straightback to strap on the calf-sheath. He paused before inserting the stiletto and stared thoughtfully at it. He wondered if when they met face-to-face he could get close enough to slice open Boss' throat? Dismissing the thought, he stood and went to his horse.

Ramon leaned on the hay cart, Jorge and Chico stood

nearby. None moved as Fargo mounted up, neither did any speak. Fargo looked at Jorge and said, "*Mucho gracias, amigo*, for bandaging my wound."

Jorge acknowledged with one slight nod.

Then Fargo shifted his gaze to Ramon and said, "Thanks for getting my horse ready to ride."

Jorge just continued to look at him.

As Fargo nudged the Ovaro to walk, he looked at Chico and leveled a promise. "I know you're wondering if my continued presence might, in some way, bring the butchers back. It won't. When I catch up with them, and I will, I'll make them pay a terrible price for what they did here, and for what they did at the Jicarilla encampment, which brought me here in the first place." Having stated it, Fargo rode around the row of adobes to North Street. Riding toward the well, he heard doors shut in advance of him. A crowd gathered around the well looked his way only briefly before it scattered and hurried in silence away from it. As he approached, Fargo counted eleven bodies bundled for burial lying in a row. They were all small in stature, so he could not pick out Maria and Papa.

He halted the pinto at the well, dismounted and drew a pail of water to soak his matted hair and loosen the blood on his ear and neck. Then he pulled the strip of sheet from his pocket and did the best job he could of wiping off the blood.

Back in the saddle, he looked down at the eleven bundles, removed his hat, and muttered, "You, Papa, brought me from the brink of death. Maria, I know you hit me on the head with the *olla,* then dragged my unconscious body to the pile of hay and covered me with it. You did it to save your lover's life, then protected my hidden body by offering your own to the Anglos. You paid a terrible price. To all of you, I say, vengeance is mine to exact. *Adios,* my gentle friends.''

Fargo donned his hat while riding tall in the saddle down South Street. Again, doors closed in advance of the black-and-white stallion.

At high noon, two days later, Skye Fargo rode into Tucson slumped in the saddle, weak as hell and tired beyond belief. He hadn't gotten any decent shut-eye between *villa deserto del diablo* and Tucson, only dozes, like now. He stayed in the saddle as much as possible because he needed a doctor in the worst way.

When he heard a wagon rumble toward him, he sat straight and opened his eyes. A rawboned man, gaunt of face, drove the one-horse farm wagon. Beside him sat two young boys. The man's penetrating stare aimed dead ahead, the boys watched the big man out of the corners of their eyes. Passing the wagon, Fargo shot a wink to the youngsters.

Riding on a street lined with shops, Fargo saw things hadn't changed much since he was here two years ago. Several of the names over the shops were different, and a couple of stores showed signs of fresh paint, but that was all. Two Studebaker farm wagons were parked out front of Hutchinson's Feed Store. A surrey stood out front of Ben Cutler's bank. Pedestrians walked in shade provided by roofs of shops. Shopkeepers and their customers stood at windows and watched his passage. He angled the Ovaro toward Charlie Livingston's livery.

Old man Livingston stood in the entrance, shovel in hand. He looked up as the pinto approached, tossed the shovel aside, and greeted, ''Wal, sakes alive, what have we here? Skye Fargo, I do believe. Long time, no see. Welcome back, Trailsman.'' Charlie waved him inside.

Fargo eased from his saddle. "How's life been treating you, Charlie? Good, I hope." A no-nonsense, law-and-order type, Livingston stood five, six in stocking feet and weighed 160 pounds buck naked. The sixty-four-year-old man still had a mouthful of teeth, a bushy, brown beard flecked with gray, and a mustache that matched. Clear brown eyes straddled a beak nose. He wore old clothes, the pants held up by red suspenders. Charlie Livingston looked like a no-good, worthless drifter. At last count, Fargo knew for a fact the old man had $2,500 in Cutler's bank. He was far from being a drifter.

"Tolerable," Charlie replied. "Staying long?"

"Figured on it. For the winter at least."

Charlie nodded toward the stalls. "Just finished cleaning 'em out. C'mon. I'll let you have your pick."

Fargo chose the last stall in a row of six. They chatted while Fargo relieved the Ovaro of his burden. "Any ruffians in town?" Fargo inquired. There had been in '58. The Dawson brothers, Luke and Harvey, shot six big men in a blazing gunfight inside Rod Mitchell's saloon on the southwest corner of Main and Cactus. All six went to Boot Hill. Three days later, Luke and Harvey joined them. And so it went.

Charlie chuckled. "Not since Abel Poteet became sheriff. Abel's got rules against that kind of thing. Enforces 'em, too. You gotta meet him."

Fargo led the stallion into the stall. Coming back to the gate, he said, "Give him good oats, all the hay and water he wants." Swinging the gate shut, he offered, "I know Abel. That's why I'm here. Figured to look in on him. Where do I put my saddle and other stuff?"

"Same place as before," Charlie said, nodding toward the tack room adjacent to the cubby hole he called his office. He picked up the bedroll and saddlebags and headed for the tack room. "Want me to clean and dress down your saddle and tack in my spare time?"

Fargo nodded. The old man's reputation for being the absolute best cleaner-upper and dresser-downer was well known to ranchers and wranglers in these parts. Fargo put his saddle astride a saddle tree, then asked, "Doc McPherson still in town?"

"Yeah, Chance is still patching people up. Why?" Charlie scanned Fargo from head to toe. "You don't look sick—wait a minute! Big man, that holster of yours is empty!" Charlie glanced at the saddlecase. "Your Sharps is also missing. You wounded?"

"Yep. Twice, at different times and places." Fargo went on to tell him what happened. "They also took what little cash I had in my hip pocket, but missed the folding money in my left boot."

"You need a loan? I got plenty in the bank."

Fargo answered through an easy grin, "Not necessary, but thanks, anyway."

Charlie walked with him as far as the gaping entrance to the livery, where they shook hands. Charlie watched the big man amble away, heading for Doc McPherson's office nestled between shops down Main. The office was handy to Mitchell's saloon, where most of Doc's more urgent business came from, and where Doc spent most of his free time drinking whiskey.

Fargo found a girl of about twelve standing between Doc's legs with her mouth wide open and him holding her tongue down with a skinny, flat stick while he peered inside. The girl's nervous mother stood nearby to watch. No one noticed Fargo enter and take a seat.

Doc removed the stick, tossed it in a wastebasket, then gave the mother his prognosis. "Your daughter is going to survive, Mrs. Bullard.'' As she heaved a sigh of relief, McPherson continued, ''But Wilma's tonsils have to come out.''

''Will it hurt?'' Wilma whined.

''Of course.'' McPherson was noted for not lying. He glanced at the worried expression on Mrs. Bullard's face and said, ''Give her a teaspoon of this three times a day, then bring her back at noon tomorrow and I'll carve them out.'' He gave her mother a small bottle of dark liquid. Wilma started bawling. Doc McPherson hurried to say, ''Good day, madam.''

As they were leaving, Doc noticed Fargo and flinched. ''God amighty, Fargo, what brings you to Tucson?'' He stood and stuck out his hand.

Shaking it, Fargo said, ''I see you are still leveling with your patients. Glad to be back, Doc.''

''No sense in lying. Tonsilectomy hurts like hell, sore after its done. Yours need removing? I can take them out right after Wilma loses hers.''

Fargo sat on the examining table and removed his shirt. McPherson started removing Jorge's bandaging job. As he did, Fargo studied him. McPherson, a tad younger than Charlie, stood five feet, ten inches and carried about an even two hundred pounds of weight. Clean-shaven, he had a square jawline and the beginning of a double-chin. Gentle gray eyes focused on the bandages. He wore a white shirt and black trousers, also held up by red suspenders. In no way did he look like a drifter.

Bandages removed, Doc inspected the place where the bullet had entered. He muttered more to himself than Fargo, ''Doesn't look too bad. Sore as hell, I guess.'' He glanced into Fargo's eyes and asked, ''When did he shoot you?''

''Couple of nights ago.'' Fargo related the circumstances. Doc moved to the other side of the table. Fargo felt his fingers touch the arrowhead wound. Doc commented, "Jesus Christ, Fargo, you're full of holes. I see where the bullet came out, but what caused where I'm feeling?"

"A Jicarilla arrow." He went on to explain the circumstances and his delirium. "An old Mexican man got the point out." He dug down in the pocket and pulled out the point and handed it to Doc.

Doc mused aloud, "I bet it felt like a big rock inside you. No wonder it brought on delirium. The old man did a good job patching you up. It's healing, so I won't mess with it. I'll clean the bullet holes with alcohol, swab 'em with a new salve from back East, then leave the bandage off so the holes can dry and scab over. When they do, don't pick at them. You listening, Fargo?"

"Heard every word. How soon do you reckon I'll be up to full speed?"

Doc came around the table to a cabinet, where he got a bottle of alcohol and a bowl of cotton. Cleaning the holes, he answered, "Healthy man like you, I'd say a week to ten days should do it. Providing you don't do anything to aggravate the two wounds."

"Not figuring on doing much of anything, anyhow, Doc."

Spreading on the salve, Doc asked, "Then why did you inquire?"

Fargo told him about the vow he made, then said, "That's why. Right now it hurts to twist. And I can count on doing a lot of fast twisting and rolling. Can't do either easily in this condition, not that it matters, but you never know. I'm having a run of back luck."

"Have no fear. If they come to Tucson, Sheriff Poteet will leave the sonsabitches' corpses lying in the street for Unk Taylor to take to Boot Hill. Put your shirt on. That'll cost you one dollar plus a glass of red-eye at Mitch's saloon."

"The drink will have to wait. Catch you later, Doc. I have

to check into the hotel first, then pay Abel a visit.'' He stepped off the examining table and twisted slowly to find the point where the pain prevented him moving any further. He found the pain erupted quickly, short of a half twist. He sat back down and took off his hat. "Look at my noggin, Doc.''

"Jesus Christ, do you have a head wound, too?'' He searched through Fargo's hair and found it. "You have a one-incher on the crown. What caused it?''

He told him about Maria hitting him with the *olla.*

"Damn, Fargo, you really got beat up coming here. I would have made a mint patching you up if I'd been handy. It's crusted over, so my services are not required. However," he paused to crack a grin, "it will cost you a second drink for me looking at it.''

Fargo handed him a dollar bill, saying, "Thanks, Doc. I'll meet you in the saloon shortly.'' Fargo put on his hat while walking to the door.

Outside on the porch, he paused to scan up and down the street. Only four horses stood hitched to rails at Mitchell's Saloon on the corner. Catty-corner from the saloon stood Gus Schmidt's two-story hotel, the Four Aces. He didn't see any horses out front, nor any people coming or going. "Quiet," he muttered. "Too damn quiet." He went to the hotel.

Gus slouched sound asleep and snoring in a red, leather chair across from his registration counter when Fargo walked into the small lobby. He said nothing as he looked at the 45-year-old hotel owner from Brooklyn in New York City. Gus was not his first name. Fargo hadn't heard his real first name. Everyone called him Gus. Gus had said a St. Louis whore pinned the name of him when he was drifting west twenty years ago. She told him he looked like a Gus. Schmidt liked the ring of it, and started going by the name. How the portly, balding man came to end up in Tucson was a mystery to Fargo. He did know how he came to own the hotel. Gus Schmidt had held all four aces, and the previous owner had held all four kings.

Fargo tapped Gus' right foot with a boot tip.

Schmidt jerked awake, half-shouted, "Don't shoot!"

Fargo grinned. Gus' face turned beet-red. He mumbled, "I had a bad dream."

"Uh, huh. I know what you mean. Had a few myself here lately. Got a room for me?"

Gus stood, stretched and yawned, then went behind the counter. He said. "Skye Fargo, it's time you settled down and quit being a Trailsman. The frontier is shrinking around you. Don't you know that?"

Schmidt had tried to sell the hotel from the moment he won it, and Fargo knew it. He'd heard those same words roll off Gus' tongue before and knew what his answer would be when he asked, "What do you have in mind, Gus?"

"You need to buy property. Property such as this hotel. I'm getting too old to run it. Young man like you ought to own it. I'll sell cheap."

Fargo nodded toward the room keys that hung from pegs on the wall behind the counter. "I'll take number nine, Gus."

Gus shook his head and handed him the key. Only then did he ask, "What brings you to our fair city?"

"Sheriff Poteet. He's a friend of mine."

"Fine man, Poteet. Remember where the toilet is?"

"Down the outside stairs and out back." Fargo slid him a wink and went upstairs to his room. He found it was stuffy. Fargo raised the window and leaned out to get a breath of fresh air. He took this room on purpose. It gave a good view of the intersection, and when leaning out the window, one could see both ends of town on Main. More than one man coming out of the saloon had been dry-gulched from Room

9 at the Four Aces Hotel. His gaze moved to the building adjacent to the saloon on Cactus. Tall white letters painted on the false front read: BUTTERFIELD STAGE. "That's new," he muttered. He left the window open to air out the room, then used the outside stairs to get on Main, where he headed for the Tucson sheriff's office and jail up Main a short distance.

As he approached, Fargo saw two saddled horses hitched to posts in front. He recognized Poteet's big dappled gray mare easy enough, and the chestnut gelding looked familiar, but he couldn't place where he had seen it. He yanked the door open and shouted, "Hands up!"

Both men instantly dropped to the floor, rolled away with their guns drawn and triggers cocked, aimed at Fargo's heart. He raised his hands, grinned and said, "Just kidding, fellows. Just kidding."

"Dammit, Fargo, you nearly got killed," Abel offered.

Roy Ballas, the easy-to-make blush, baby-faced Texan, better known as Kid Ballas, blushed as he stood and holstered his ivory-gripped Smith & Wesson.

Fargo stepped to and gave Roy a manly embrace. "Kid, I thought I saw your horse outside, but wasn't sure. When did you come to Tucson?"

"Shortly after my wife, Vanessa, was murdered by a person or persons unknown. Without her, my life wasn't the same. So I pinned my sheriff's badge on Mozart Higgins' shirt and moved on. Ended up here."

Pouring a cup of coffee, Abel added, "Good for me that he did. Kid's my deputy." He handed the cup to Fargo.

"Well, Abel, you got the best. But I think you know that." Fargo looked into Abel Poteet's steel-blue eyes that had backed down more than one drawn six-shooter. At age fifty, Abel still had one of the fastest draws Fargo had seen. Tall and rough-cut handsome, the tobacco-chewing man had the reputation of spitting on the gun pointed at him. Caught by surprise, the gunman would blink. When he did, Abel would knock the gun out of the man's hand, then haul him to jail. Few men argued with the still muscular two-hundred-pounder and his Colt, identical to the one missing from Fargo's holster.

Abel noticed its absence. His eyes kicked up to Fargo's when he inquired, "I see you have your Colt in for repair at Dick Cottingham's gun store. What's wrong with it?"

"Not at Dick's place. I don't know where it is, yet." He went on to explain the circumstances surrounding how he lost it and his Sharps.

Both Abel and Kid shook their heads, then Abel said, "I have a drawer full of revolvers their owners have no further use for." Abel pulled open the bottom drawer of his desk and said, "Take your pick. Rifles are in the rack. No Sharps, though."

The drawer was all but overflowing with handguns. Fargo rummaged through them and saw six single action, five-shot Remington-Beals pocket revolvers with brass trigger guards, three short-barreled rimfire pistols, two seven-shot, single action Model One Smith & Wessons, two Smith & Wesson Army issues, like Kit toted, minus his ivory grips, and one single action Colt Navy Model that had a cracked frame. The rest were belt pistols having rounded trigger guards and loading levers. Fargo took one of the Smith & Wesson Army issues, put it in his holster, then whipped it out a few times to get the feel.

Kid commented, "Slow, Mr. Fargo. I know your Colt comes out faster."

Abel suggested, "Doesn't matter. He won't have to draw it, anyhow. Fargo, do you think those butchers are headed this way?"

"Could be. If you project their known path."

Abel pulled open a top drawer and gave Fargo a handful of cartridges for the Smith & Wesson. "If you're right, you might need these after all. Want a rifle?"

"No. Maybe later, but not now."

Business aside, they sat to drink Abel's coffee and catch up on one another. Evening shadows crept through the windows before they finished. Abel pushed back from his desk and stepped into the doorway. Fargo and Kid watched him scan up and down the street. "Looks quiet enough," Abel tossed over his shoulder. "You men want to join me for supper at the cafe?"

Fargo and Kid exchanged glances and shrugs. Fargo asked, "Poteet, are you paying?" He threw Kid a wink.

"Hell, no!" Abel shot back. "I'll pay for the first cup of coffee."

"He's a hard man, Mr. Fargo," Kid said through a grin. "Tight-fisted, too."

They went outside so Poteet could lock up, then walked shoulder to shoulder in the middle of Main, Kid between the taller two. Kid commented, "If a stranger in town saw us, they would think we are gunslingers on the prowl."

Fargo and Poteet chuckled. A stride later, Poteet tripped Kid. "You stumbling on your shadow again, Kid?" Poteet muttered.

At the cafe, they ate some of Lillian Clarke's roast beef with trimmings while her husband, George, all but drowned them with his coffee. When Fargo asked who was new in town, both lawmen knew what he meant. Abel replied, "We have been keeping an eye on three at Mitchell's saloon."

Kid picked up on it from there. "Gunslingers for hire if I ever saw one. But, so far they've been quiet as church mice. Not one bit of trouble. In fact, one is a friendly cuss. Easy to smile and crack jokes."

"Deadly," Fargo grunted.

"I don't think they knew one another before coming to Tucson," Abel suggested. "They drifted in from different directions and at different times. Told me they were here to kill time and play poker."

"Reckon they are in the saloon, now?" Fargo asked. He watched both men nod, then said, "I'm going to the saloon when we leave here. I owe Doc McPherson a couple of whiskeys. If he hasn't changed his drinking habits, Doc will still be there."

"No change," Abel replied.

Fargo asked, "Do you know their names?"

"Yep," Abel began. "Bucky Mullins, Glenn Bassett and Sanford McCord."

Kid added, "McCord is the friendly one. He goes by Pinky."

"I know Pinky McCord," Fargo said. "You said it right, Kid, Pinky's gun's for hire. So are his fists. I watched him beat three big men half to death one night in a Wichita saloon. I heard he fought for money back East. He's mean and he's tough as an old boot."

"You'll know Bassett when you see him," Abel said. "He'll be the one with a bullwhip coiled around his left shoulder."

Fargo nodded. "Who else is new in town?"

Abel replied, "Other than two worthless drifters, no one else."

Kid offered, "Yesterday 'bout four in the afternoon, while at the smithy, I watched a duster-clad drifter ride in from the north. He stopped for Lloyd to fit a new shoe on his horse."

Fargo's eyes narrowed as he asked, "Which hoof?"

Kid answered, "Hind left."

4

"Did you get a good look at him?" Fargo asked, now certain the man rode with Boss' butchers.

"Like I said, he wore a duster. The beady-eyed no-good showed me a mouthful of rotted teeth when he smiled and stuck out his dirty hand to me. He told me his name and where he came from. He saw my deputy badge, of course, and said he wasn't in town to cause any trouble, only to get a new shoe, then he'd be moseying on."

Fargo's hopes soared that the no-good would prove to be Boss. "What's his name, Kid?"

"Otis Earl Puckett. Claimed he and four others had struck it rich in Colorado, but an early, heavy snowfall ran them out of the high country before they could open their gold mine. He paid Lloyd with a tiny nugget. I assumed he wasn't lying."

"His voice?" Fargo asked.

"High-pitched. Whiny. You know the kind."

Fargo did, indeed. Otis Earl had handed Boss Fargo's Colt. "Did you notice the direction he went after Lloyd finished?"

Kid shook his head. "I had other things to do, so I left before Lloyd got through."

"Then you don't know if Otis left town," Fargo suggested.

"That's true,," Kid replied. "But I didn't see him in town

after leaving Lloyd's place. Nor have I seen him today. Abel, have you seen him?''

"No one that fits your description of him is in Tucson," Abel answered. "I would have spotted him for damn sure," he added flatly.

"What kind of horse was Otis Earl on?" Fargo asked. He needed all the information he could get.

"Underfed dun mare. She already had her winter coat, which further led me to believe that Otis had just come from cold country and had not lied."

Fargo probed deeper into Kid's memory. "Did he say who the others were, mention any of their names, or how many? I think you shook hands with the butcher's scout, but I want to make sure."

Kid shook his head. "No. All he said was others."

Fargo's plate was clean, his remaining coffee cold. There was nothing more to be said. He wiped his mouth with his napkin, then rose from the chair and allowed he was going to the saloon and pay his debt to Doc. Kid said he would see him there later, after Poteet and he had made their rounds. Fargo left them sitting there, drinking coffee.

As always, he paused outside the double-doors of the saloon to scan inside. He saw no signs of trouble while scanning the thirteen men and one woman in the smoky room. He recognized six.

Heavyset, short-bearded Ben Cutler, owner of the bank, stood at the near end of the long bar. Ben stared thoughtfully into the mug of beer before him.

Next to Ben stood three dusty wranglers Fargo didn't know. But he did know the raven-haired, shapely saloon girl standing with them. Fargo had visited Viola's room out back several times in the past.

Down a ways from the wranglers stood Doc. Doc gripped

a glass of whiskey tightly, as though it might get away from him. He chatted with Raymond Simmons, the bartender. Raymond nodded at all the right times, as though he had heard it before.

Next to Doc was a man who Fargo didn't recognize. A wiry, intense fellow with brown pork-chop sideburns, he wore a dark-brown vest and toted a big Navy Colt. He rested his back to the bar and watched two men who sat across the table from one another drinking beer. Fargo did not recognize the pair.

At the far end of the bar, facing Fargo, stood Glenn Bassett, identifiable by the bullwhip coiled around his left shoulder, like Kid had mentioned. A lean man—Fargo reckoned him about thirty—Bassett stood five, ten, and had red, curly hair and a gambler's mustache. He, too, wore a leather vest, albeit jet-black. Bassett had a shot glass in front of him.

McCord, Mitchell, and Alan Moore, who owned the General Store, sat at the table in the far corner of the saloon across from the bar. They held cards. McCord had the seat in the corner, where he could see everyone in the room and watch the double-doors.

Fargo pushed inside. McCord's eyes cut from his cards to him. They acknowledged each other with nods so slight no one except Bassett noticed. Bassett's glance from Fargo to McCord and back again happened so fast no one except Fargo noticed.

Viola looked into the long mirror behind the bar now and then, and Fargo knew it. "Checking up," she called it. By that Viola meant she looked to see if a "prospect"—and all men fell into that category—had entered so quietly that he had gone unnoticed by her. Fargo walked right past her and bellied-up to the bar to the right of Doc before she checked and saw him. Viola instantly lost all interest in the wranglers and came smiling to Fargo. She wedged between him and Doc, leaned her back to the bar, looked Fargo straight in the eye, and said, "It's been a hell of a long time since I last looked into those lake-blues."

"How are you doing, honey?" Fargo inquired.

She showed him a rocking hand gesture, smirked, "Give away about as much as I get paid for."

Fargo kissed her, patted her fanny, then said, "Maybe later, honey. Right now Doc and I have some serious drinking to do."

"Promise?" Viola asked. "It's free to you. You know that."

Fargo nodded. Viola returned to the wranglers. Raymond stuck out his hand to Fargo. "Welcome back, Fargo," he greeted.

A roly-poly sort, Raymond had the honor of having been the saloon's only bartender since Doug Horton built it. Since then, Raymond had survived four owners for the same reason; Raymond didn't take shit from any customer, or anyone else. You could get away with calling Raymond a hard name, but you better not lay hands on him or say he shorted you on a drink. If you committed either of the last two heinous crimes, Raymond took it personal and the next thing you saw were the double-barrels of his shotgun aimed between your eyes. Fargo liked the man, respected him. So, he warmly shook Raymond's hand, saying, "My pleasure, Ray. Have you had to show old Betsy to anyone lately?"

"Nope. Not since Poteet got voted in as sheriff. First one is on the house. What'll it be? Bourbon?"

Fargo nodded. "And I'm buying Doc, here, two refills."

"I'll drink to that," Doc said jovially.

Raymond poured, then moved to the wranglers. Doc took to mumbling to himself—something about leaving Tucson for good—and Fargo put his wild-creature to work, eavesdropping on the two men at the table, while he studied their reflections in the mirror. They were leaning toward one another, talking in low tones, as though conspiring. Fargo guessed both were thirty. They weren't wranglers or ranchers, nor were they businessmen or drummers. And they certainly were not lawmen. Fargo decided they were the two drifters. He heard the heavier man call the other one Leland, and Leland call him E.C. twice and Harper once. He didn't catch their subject, because Doc's elbow nudged him and broke the concentration. Fargo loooked at Doc and said, "Hell, Doc, you've been leaving Tucson ever since I first met you."

"You haven't heard a word I said, have you?"

"Uh, refresh my memory." Fargo laid it off on the pain in his shoulder, which was sore as hell.

"I was saying I might buy Schmidt's hotel. If I'm going to stay here, I might as well invest some of my money in property. What do you think?"

Again, Fargo caught only a word or two from what Doc said, enough to catch his drift. Fargo was watching the poker player's reflection in the mirror, waiting for a shuffle-up. Mitchell pulled the pot in. Alan started shuffling the deck. Fargo said, "Wise move, Doc," then took his drink and moseyed to the poker table, where all three men paused to exchange greetings with him.

Mitchell offered, "Pull back a chair, Fargo, and sit a spell. This is an open game. Five card stud."

"Thanks, but I'm leaving shortly," Fargo apologized.

"Leaving town, or just for the night?" Mitchell glanced at Viola.

"For the night. *Alone* in my room," Fargo was quick to say.

Pinky asked, "What brings you to Tucson?"

Fargo grinned. "Cold weather chased me out of Colorado high country."

Now Pinky grinned. "Hell, Trailsman, I thought you enjoyed being snowbound. You still ride that pretty pinto stallion? Wouldn't want to sell him by any chance?"

"Not for sale or trade, Pinky. What's your friends' names? The two standing at the bar, wearing vests?" Fargo spoke just loud enough so they would hear if eavesdropping.

Pinky and Mitchell glanced toward them, then Pinky replied, "Don't know 'em."

Bassett said, "I'm Glenn Bassett. I'm out of Texas. What else do you want to know about me?"

Fargo noticed Bassett spoke baritone in a near whisper, kinda slow and easy like. No drawl, though.

Then quick on Bassett's words, the other man identified himself. "Name's Bucky Mullins, out of Carson Valley. What's yours? I already know the where."

"Skye Fargo."

"Relax, men," Pinky said. "Fargo and I go way back. He's all right. If you don't cross him, that is. Then he's hell on wheels, whether it be guns, fists, or knives." Pinky was letting them know what most of the men and Viola already knew—that Fargo could be deadly when provoked.

Bucky and Bassett went back to drinking. The two drifters had slipped out the swinging door during the brief dialogue.

Raymond kept the liquor flowing while Fargo watched six hands of draw play out. The threesome won two hands each. During the sixth hand, Viola led a wrangler out back. During the shuffle, Kid walked in, followed by the two drifters. The drifters sat at the same table as before. Kid came to the poker game and sat to watch with Fargo.

Fargo asked, "Anything going on, Kid?"

"Naw. All's quiet. Poteet stopped at the office to catch up on paperwork. Who's winning?"

"Me," all three poker players chorused. That brought belly laughs from as far away as Raymond behind the bar, including Bassett and Bucky.

Raymond poured Kid, a nondrinker, a glass of sarsaparilla and brought it to him. Kid took a sip, then asked if Fargo's shoulder hurt too bad to play cards. All three players looked at Fargo.

Alan asked, "You're hurt?"

"Caught a Jicarilla arrow north of here," Fargo explained. "If that wasn't bad enough, someone shot me in the same shoulder two nights ago and left me for dead."

"Did you see who shot you?" Pinky asked the question.

Fargo sheepishly admitted, "No. She had already knocked me unconscious."

"She?" Mitchell half hollered, then burst out laughing.

Fargo was in too deep now to stop. If Mitchell didn't drag it out of him, he thought, McCord would. So, Fargo told all, including losing his guns to a man called Boss.

When he was through, Pinky commented, "Shit, Fargo, you're in one hell of a bad fix. Wounds in the head and in the shoulder, borrowed six-gun, no rifle—did they steal your money, too?"

"Only what they found in my pockets."

"You better get some shut-eye, pardner," Mitchell recommended. "After all that, you've been in the saddle two straight days. You need rest, Fargo. Good rest."

They went back to playing cards. Fargo watched two deals play out before he stood to leave. He asked Kid, "It's none of my business, but where are you staying?"

"With the new preacher and his family, Silas Beauchamp. Miss Katie, she's their eldest, sixteen going on seventeen, she's teaching me how to play chess. She plays the piano at church services, too."

"Sounds like Miss Katie is an all-around young lady. You taking a fancy to her?"

Kid blushed. "Aw, Mr. Fargo, she's just a snip of a girl."

"Are you going to get a chess lesson tonight?" Fargo was funning with the blushing young Texan. He knew the players were listening. Alan Moore, especially, would rib Kid now that he knew about Kid having eyes for the preacher's daughter. It would be all over Tucson in no time flat.

"Too late. Her mother makes Katie go to bed with the chickens. Mr. Fargo, you wouldn't want to attend church services with me in the morning, would you? I'd be pleased if you did."

"If I feel up to it. You staying or going home?"

"Thought I might watch for a spell longer."

Fargo nodded. "Well, goodnight, gents. See you in church." As he walked away, he heard the poker players mumble incoherently. Fargo grinned.

Heading to the hotel across the intersection, he saw three horses hitched out front. That told him the guests were overnighters. None of the horses were duns. Upon entering the lobby, he didn't see Gus, but saw his little sign that read RING FOR SERVICE and bell next to the registration book on the counter. Halfway to the stairs, Fargo paused and looked at the registration book. He went over and opened it. Below his name were the names E. C. Harper, Leland Baird, and Judge Helton Smith. All had rooms on the ground floor. Fargo closed the book and went to his room, undressed and stretched out on the bed. He drifted into sleep staring at the ceiling.

Two back-to-back gunshots jerked him awake. Gun in hand, Fargo rolled out of bed. Two strides put him at the window. He leaned out and saw Kid blast through the swinging doors, gripping his weapon. Fargo shouted to him, "Up Main! Far end!" Kid Ballas ran up Main as the saloon emptied and rushed to follow. Fargo dressed and ran downstairs. Gus and Judge Smith stood in their underwear on the hotel porch, looking up Main. Fargo sprinted past them, headed that way.

He saw the saloon crowd gathered outside the livery entrance. Kid knelt at a man's body. Fargo slowed to a walk as he pushed between Mitchell and Leland Baird. Sheriff Poteet lay dead in a puddle of blood from two bullet holes in his back. "Was Abel alive when you got to him?" Fargo asked short of breath.

"Barely," Kid answered. He stood and added, "Otis Earl dry-gulched him from inside the livery. Abel had the drop on your man Boss."

Ben Cutler came out of the livery and said, "Charlie's dead, too. Throat cut, belly layed open. Gruesome sight."

Other townsmen joined those from the saloon as most of them moved inside to see the butchery. Kid singled out ten men for his posse. Fargo wasn't one of them. Kid explained to him why. "You're the best tracker I know, Mr. Fargo. But you're a wounded man. That has to affect your timing. You're exhausted. That has to affect your alertness. And you have never fired that Smith and Wesson. Sorry, Mr. Fargo, but I can't take you."

Fargo nodded. Kid was now in charge and had every right to choose who rode with him.

Kid said to his posse, "Get your horses and rifles. Assemble at the sheriff's office in ten minutes. Be prepared to ride all night."

Those in the posse hurried away. Solemn-faced, Unk Taylor appeared. Kid told him to take the bodies to the funeral parlor. "You can bury them after the posse returns."

Unk nodded.

Fargo walked with Kid to the office, where Kid took a breech-loading Henry from the rack and a pocketful of cartridges for it from a desk drawer. Glumly, he muttered, "Mr. Fargo, why do decent, law-abiding people have to die?"

"Kid, decent, law-abiding people have pondered that same question since the beginning of time. I don't know the answer."

"I suppose you're right, Mr. Fargo. Good versus evil is a never-ending struggle.'"

Fargo followed him outside, where four mounted men in the posse waited. Two others rode up from behind the office as Kid mounted up. Fargo saw the others coming up Main. When they arrived he told them, "Good hunting. Kid, don't forget to retrieve my Colt and Sharps."

Kid nodded. Fargo watched him lead the posse north, into the night, then he walked back to the hotel. Fargo undressed, reclined in the bed, and stared at the ceiling a second time this night. Sleep came quickly this time. Fargo was, indeed, exhausted. And his shoulder did hurt.

At mid-morning, a loud shout from in the street stirred him awake. The voice shouted again, "Posse coming! Posse coming!" Fargo stepped to the window and leaned out. Strung out in an irregular column from the north end of town came the weary posse. The horses appeared as tired as the men. Kid didn't notice Fargo until he approached below the window. Kid shook his head slowly. Then he called up to him, "We're going to the church to have a town meeting." As soon as he finished saying that the church bell began to ring.

Fargo nodded. He washed up, pulled on his clothes, then

left. He followed Alan Moore, the last rider in the posse, to the church. As Alan dismounted, Fargo caught up with him and asked, "Did you men even see them?"

Alan shook his head.

Fargo knew that people in Tucson congregated in one of three places—Alan Moore's General Store, Rod Mitchell's saloon, and Brother Silas Beauchamp's nondenominational God's Only Church In Tucson. Those were the only three structures spacious enough to accommodate a gathering. For small crowds that included females, Moore's place was used. Men-only crowds usually met in the saloon. The church had room and pews enough to handle sizable crowds. Seemed to Fargo as though the entire population of Tucson attended church this morning. The sanctuary was packed; men stood at open windows and the open front door. Others milled about on the church grounds or among the many wagons, buggies, and surreys.

Fargo joined those men knotted at windows. He looked over their shoulders and saw two coffins in front of the altar. Beauchamp and Roy Ballas stood nearby. Abel Poteet's coffin was open. The lid of Charlie's had been nailed shut. Men lined all four walls. Two open graves were in the back part of the cemetery behind Fargo.

Reverend Beauchamp spoke: "Friends, we are gathered here in God's house to pay our last respects to these two God-fearing men. That has been done, so no more words are to be said over them. As you see, Deputy Ballas and his posse have returned. Deputy Ballas has something to say. Deputy, go ahead."

Kid looked at Abel. In a cracked voice he said, "Sheriff, Charlie, we failed to catch your murderers. I'm sorry." Collecting himself, he now looked at the people in the room. Strengthening his voice, he said, "Before he died in my arms, Abel said to tell you people he believed Mr. Skye Fargo would be your best choice to replace him. And I agree. So . . ." Kid paused to scan the room and find Fargo.

Ben Cutler stood at the wall opposite from the window where Fargo stood. Pointing to the window, Ben said, "Fargo's outside, looking in, deputy."

Heads turned to face the window. Kid said, "Mr. Fargo, please come stand beside me so everyone can get a good look at their new sheriff."

Reluctantly, Fargo went inside and stood next to Kid. Fargo's gun hand stroked his short beard as he carefully chose the words to say he didn't want the job. After the long pause, he said, "I'm tempted, yes, for several good reasons. Uppermost is, Abel Poteet was my friend. I would do most anything for him. Second, these devil-butchers must be brought to justice. However, I am compelled to refuse Abel's badge of office for several good reasons. Let me explain. First, I have personal reasons to catch the culprits. I must be free to track them down, wherever they go. In that context, I would be a part-time sheriff. You folks deserve a full-time sheriff. Second, I'm a wounded man. Simply put, I'm not yet physically sound enough to function as your sheriff. If a problem arose that called for gunplay, in my condition I would probably get killed. That is the main reason that stopped me from going with the posse. I suggest you good people select Roy Ballas to wear the sheriff's badge."

The congregation fairly buzzed with the babble of conversation. A man said he thought Kid was too young to be a sheriff. Another claimed Kid was inexperienced for the job. A woman said he wasn't tall enough. Another voiced he was too new in town. A man seated in the rear pew said Kid led the posse on a wild goose chase . . . and so it went.

Only when Fargo stepped off the platform and reached a hand into Abel's coffin did a hush fall over the room. He removed the sheriff's badge from Abel's vest and then returned to the platform. Grim-jawed, Fargo told the naysayers in the crowd, "Honor my recommendation. Ballas is the best you have."

Doc McPherson shouted, "Pin it on him, Fargo!"

Judge Smith rose from a pew across the aisle from McPherson. Although he spoke only four words, his rich baritone voice uttered most eloquently and with unshakable authority: "I second that motion."

Beauchamp thundered, "All in favor say aye!"

The sanctuary vibrated with ayes.

Lowering his voice, Beauchamp's eyes were in constant movement as he said, "All against making Roy the sheriff of Tucson, say nay."

With tears streaming down her face, Katie Beauchamp rose off her piano bench. In a trembly voice she voiced the only nay.

Fargo knew why. Katie didn't want Kid involved in gunplay.

Kid turned to face her. Solemn faced he said, "Miss Katie, I have to."

Fargo removed Kid's deputy badge, handed it to him, then pinned on the sheriff's badge. Shaking Kid's hand, Fargo told him, "Wear it proudly, Sheriff Ballas, wear it long."

"I will," Kid replied.

Those seated rearranged their bottoms on the hard pews. Those standing shifted weight to their other foot. No one said anything. There was no more to be said on the subject. Beauchamp said, "Pallbearers, please step forward."

Fargo watched twelve men come forward. Six each hoisted the two coffins onto their shoulders and carried them outside to the open graves, where Beauchamp committed Poteet's and Livingston's souls to God Almighty. Unk Taylor nailed the lid on Poteet's coffin, then it and Livingston's were lowered to the bottom of the graves. Four men put shovels to work and sealed Poteet's and Charlie's bodies in peaceful darkness forevermore.

It was over. It was high noon in Tucson. Everyone went home—Kid with an arm around Katie's waist. Fargo walked alone to the hotel.

In his room, he lay on his stomach in bed and stared out the window. The hairs on his nape started to tingle. He turned his head slowly and looked at the door. It wasn't ajar. Neither was the knob being quietly turned. He listened for a movement out in the hall and heard none. He faced the window again. He heard no sounds come from the street below. His eyes started to close, but he jerked them open again and muttered, "No. Go look."

At the window, Fargo rubbed the back of his neck while he studied the street and intersection. His gaze inexorably shifted to the saloon. He saw six horses hitched to the rail on the Main Street side of the saloon. Two he had seen the night before hitched at the hotel. He started to look away, then something caught his eye, a movement in the narrow space between the saloon and barbershop on Main. He focused on the space. A horse's dark tail swished. A mare backed her rump out the scant opening.

She was a dun.

ing at her brother's angry, sweating face as it rose toward the intersection. Heavy brows over a haversack were his eyes. The Butte field couldn't make him father if her brother let it.

5

Skye Fargo hurried down the stairs and went outside. The streets were deserted except for the horses at the saloon. Fargo strode straight across the intersection to the walkspace where he had seen the dun mare. He looked in. Ground reined, the mare was free to move backward and forward. She was doing both. Fargo talked to and touched the mare so she would know he was behind her and not spook. He raised her left hind hoof and looked at the shoe. Then he moved to the right hind hoof and looked at that shoe. There was no doubt in Fargo's mind that the dun belonged to Otis Earl.

Satisfied, he stepped onto the saloon's porch and peered around the near side of a window. Raymond was behind the bar. The three gunslingers were shoulder to shoulder across the bar from him. Pinky and Glenn were talking, while Bucky looked in the mirror. Five men sat around the poker table in the corner. Leland and E. C. sat with their backs to Fargo. Duster-clad Otis Earl sat at Leland's left, his profile to Fargo. A lean man—Fargo guessed his age at twenty-two, give or take a year—sat at E.C.'s right. A dough-faced, much older man—Fargo reckoned him to be mid-fifty—sat with his back to the corner so he could see the front door. Dough-face, a big bruiser, looked mean-tough. That would be Boss, Fargo reckoned. He didn't see Viola or any of the wranglers, and presumed that she was still taking care of their needs.

A stagecoach rumbled at high-speed behind Fargo, heading toward the intersection. He saw Boss track its passage with his eyes. The Butterfield celerity skidded into Cactus Street and slowed, leaving a great cloud of swirling dust in the intersection.

Fargo moved to the swinging-doors and looked inside over them. He had no intention of entering. He wanted Boss to see him. Boss cut his eyes away from the celerity, back to the double-doors. Fargo saw him visibly tense. Boss had seen him all right and recognized him. That was good enough for Fargo. With his eyes drilling into Boss's, Fargo backed off the porch, then turned and ambled to the middle of the dusty intersection, where he turned to face the double-doors.

Consumed in the slowly settling dust, Fargo parted his feet and waited for the butchers to come out. In his peripheral vision, through the dust, he saw the stage driver hand a suitcase to a female passenger, then the woman walked toward him. As she approached, Fargo heard someone coming from behind. His gun hand edged closer to the grip of the holstered Smith & Wesson.

Kid's voice said, "It's just me, Mr. Fargo." Kid halted a shoulder's width to the right of Fargo. Looking at the swinging doors, Kid muttered, "Are the bastards inside?"

Fargo nodded. "They're trying to figure out how to kill my ghost. Be out any second now. Kid, this fight is mine. Stop that woman. Get her out of the line of fire."

Kid ran and pulled her away from Fargo. The woman began a loud protest, "You ruffian, take your hands—!"

Glass shattered. Leland Baird crashed through a saloon window that fronted Main. A split-second later, E.C. Harper dived through the window on Cactus. Both tumbled off the porch onto the street. The man whose profile Fargo had seen charged through the swinging doors. His six-gun belched hot lead. Fargo drew down on him and fired. The man catapulted back through the double-doors.

Gun drawn, Baird scrambled to his feet. Fargo shot him in the head. A hunk of skull and bloody brains flew outward. Baird spun halfway around and fell across a hitching rail.

Harper's bullets kicked up puffs of dust between Fargo's boots. He twisted to his right and shot Harper in the heart. Harper's dead trigger finger jerked twice as he fell backward, the slugs thudded into the saloon.

Fargo glanced at the double-doors. He had bullets left for Otis Earl and Boss. It didn't look as though the cowards would come out and shoot it out with the big man. Boldly, Fargo strode for the saloon's entrance.

He was halfway there when Kid shouted, "Look left!"

Fargo halted in mid-stride as Boss stepped between the dun mare and barbershop. He held Fargo's Colt.

Three shots rang out simultaneously. Boss' bullet came so close to Fargo's head that it disturbed his hair. Fargo's bullet hit Boss in the upper right arm. He lost his grip on the Colt. Fargo watched it fall to the ground, as he felt the third bullet drill fire through his right thigh.

He twisted to his right and glimpsed Otis Earl, who stood just outside the scant opening on Cactus. As his right leg buckled, Fargo shot at him. The bullet went wild. Otis took dead aim on Fargo's head. Before Otis could cook off the killing shot, Raymond's double-barreled shotgun roared from within the opening. The tight pattern of buckshot shredded Otis Earl's head.

Fargo glanced to the opening on Main. Boss had disappeared, but Fargo's Colt had not. He hobbled to it. Picking it up, he heard hoofbeats pounding away from behind the saloon. Fargo limped as fast as he could through the opening to the rear of the saloon and barbershop. Boss leaned low over his horse's neck, too far away for the Colt's bullets to reach. Fargo holstered his Colt, then stuck the Smith & Wesson in the Levi's waistband. He turned and saw Raymond. The bartender's somber expression foretold a tragedy.

Raymond nodded toward Viola's shack and said glum-voiced, "Vi and the cowpokes are dead. Can you make it inside the saloon?"

Fargo limped to the back door. He braced on Raymond while they went to a chair. Sitting, Fargo said, "Get me something to use for a tourniquet." He started pulling off his boots and Levi's.

Doc McPherson, black medical bag in hand, came through the swinging-doors and hurried to Fargo. Inspecting the wound, Doc lamented, "A man simply cannot catch a Sunday afternoon nap for all the shooting around here." Raymond handed him a long sash.

While Doc wiped blood, Fargo looked at McCord and the others standing at the bar, watching in the mirror. McCord met Fargo's gaze and said dryly, "Good shooting, Fargo. I see you haven't lost your touch." He nodded toward the man lying on the floor with blood on his chest and added, "You shot the rascal in the heart." He and the other two gunslingers went back to drinking.

Kid Ballas came in. Looking at Fargo's wound, he asked, "Did you get all five?"

"No. Boss escaped. He rode south. With my Sharps." He watched Unk Taylor move from body to body and search each man's pockets.

Kid offered, "I got a hotel room for Mildred Gibbons."

Doc rocked back in his chair. Wiping blood off his hands, he cited his prognosis, "You will live and get to keep the leg. If the slug had gone an inch to the left, you would have lost it. Now, Fargo, I want you to stay off your feet for a week." He closed the bag and ordered a glass of whiskey. "My client will pay for it," he told Raymond.

Kid said, "I'll borrow a sheet from Viola to wrap around you. Then we will carry you to your room."

Fargo groaned at the thought of lying in bed for a week.

Raymond followed Kid out the back door. While they fetched the sheet, Mitchell, Ben Cutler, and Sam Hutchinson walked inside. Mitch went behind the bar and poured whiskey into three shot glasses, then filled a fourth with bourbon and brought all four to the table where Fargo sat. He handed two of the whiskeys to the banker and feed-store owner, and kept one for himself. Handing the shot glass of bourbon to Fargo, Mitchell said, "Thanks for not shooting up my saloon, especially the mirror. Windows can be replaced easily, but mirrors that size are hard to come by. How many did you kill? I saw Unk hauling four away."

"One fled south," Fargo answered. "What's in that general direction? Where would he go?" Fargo took a sip of bourbon.

Mitchell drank half his whiskey, then answered, "Sahuarita. Nothing but desert in between. Why? You figuring on going after him?"

"The day I feel good enough to ride."

Kid and Raymond returned with a folded sheet. Kid said, "The butchers slashed Viola's throat and three ranchhands' from old man Tucker's spread." He handed the sheet to Fargo, then asked the three gunslingers to help him carry the big man to his room.

Fargo thought they would not, but he was wrong. While carrying him to the room, they made light of Fargo letting Boss get away. Pinky started it. He joked, "That Smith and Wesson I saw you aim must have a bent barrel." That brought a chuckle from all but Fargo. He was in no mood for such talk. And Bassett noticed it. Tongue-in-cheek, he muttered dryly, "Blew off one side of that fool's head, too. Messy. You were off a tad. Should've shot him between the eyes." Bucky stepped in and added, "Aw, Glenn, his left shoulder is killing him. Ain't that right, big feller?" And so it went about Fargo's marksmanship.

Passing through the hotel lobby, they saw the Gibbons woman talking over the counter to Gus. Fargo thought she looked like a spinster schoolmarm. Thin-lipped, hard stare, hair done up in a bun, high-collar, green dress, the hem of which touched her ankles. Fargo tossed her a wink. Her face turned beet-red as she snorted, "Humph! My word! Of all the audacity!" Mildred tossed her head back.

They laid him face up on the bed. Bassett moved to the window and looked out, while Kid put Fargo's boots and bloody Levi's on the floor next to the door. Pinky said, "The three of us have bottom-floor rooms. I'll bring you a bottle of bourbon next time I come from the saloon."

Kid inquired if he needed or wanted anything now.

Fargo shook his head. "Thanks, men, for toting my sorry ass to the bed."

"Think nothing of it," Bucky replied. "It was getting kind of boring around here, anyway. Gave us something to do."

Kid said, "Well, fellows, I got to make the rounds. So I better hop to it."

Reaching for them, Kid said, "I'll take your Levi's and boots to Miss Katie."

"That's not necessary," Fargo began. "You're not fooling me, Kid. You want to make damn sure I will stay in this room."

Kid opened the door, then turned. Looking at Fargo, he explained, "Miss Katie will be honored to wash and iron the Levi's and put a shine on the boots of the man who wouldn't let her man fight it out with them. You know you wouldn't be lying there in the bed with a bullet hole in your leg if you had let me protect your blind side.''

"Kid, it wasn't your fault. I told you that.''

Kid's expression conveyed he was hurt that Fargo would say such a thing. "Oh? Sheriff Poteet was my friend, too. Charlie Livingston, also.''

Fargo put it on a more personal basis. "Kid, I know they were. All of us will miss them. But they had my guns. And they had shot me. Maybe with my own gun. So it was between them and me. Under different circumstances, I would have been proud to stand shoulder-to-shoulder with you and sling lead, shoot it out with the bastards. Take the boots and Levi's to Miss Katie. I will be honored to have her clean them.''

Kid nodded. "Okay," he said. "But I still don't feel right.'' He stepped out into the hall and pulled the door shut.

Pinky mused aloud, "Do you two always go at it like that?''

"No. Only after a hot gunfight in which one of us gets it in his head that he didn't measure up. I could have easily taken Kid's position.''

After a long moment, Pinky said, "The next time I come from the saloon I'll bring you a bottle of bourbon. I know what it feels like to be trapped inside four walls.''

Fargo knew what McCord meant. The man had languished in jails more than once for busting heads. Fargo nodded.

Bassett left the window, headed for the door. Passing the bed, he muttered, "Fargo, I would have done the same as you. Nobody takes my gun.''

Bucky, then McCord followed him out the door.

Fargo rolled over to face the window. He closed his eyes

and willed himself to ignore the pain in his thigh. Moments later he found sleep.

A rap on his door awakened him. A female voice said, "It's me, Mr. Fargo, Lillian Clarke."

Pulling the sheet up, he said, "Come in."

She backed inside. Fargo saw why. Lillian's arms were laden with food from the cafe. She smiled as she came to the table next to the bed. Skillfully, she slid a platter onto its top, then moved the lamp to one side to make room for the rest. She said, "George and I heard Doc confined you to the bed for a week or so. I'll be bringing you three hot meals each day. Fargo, we want you to get well, get your strength back as soon as possible."

Fargo looked at more food than one man could possibly eat when she removed the lids from the platters. One was filled with baked ham, yams, and red beans. Another held roast beef with trimmings. Steam rose from a bowl of chili. A small basket contained hot biscuits and wheat bread. He watched her step out into the hall, then come back carrying a coffeepot, cup, and saucer. Amazed, he said, "How in the world did you do it? Carry this much grub from the cafe, up a flight of stairs, without dropping anything?"

She laughed, "You can bet I spilled a whole lot learning how. Now, eat before your meal gets cold."

Lillian lingered at the window a short time and watched him eat her fixings, long enough to see he preferred the roast beef. "I'll take the dishes and coffeepot away when I bring breakfast. Now, make it easy on me and eat all of it. I don't want to see one smidgen left to throw to the dogs. You hear me, Fargo?"

He told himself he would do it even if he had to crawl to the back stairs and dump the leftovers to the ground below. "I hear, Lillian."

"What do you want me to fix you for breakfast?"

"I'm not fussy."

She left the window. Pointing to the bowl of chili, she said, "Don't let it turn cold."

As she brushed by the foot of his bed, Fargo dipped a spoonful of the chili.

"Good," Lillian commented as she went out the door.

He waited for her to close the door, then put the spoon back into the bowl. He muttered, "Fargo, the woman is going to make you too fat to fight." He tried the yams.

An hour after Lillian had departed, a stiff wind arose. It sent dust through the open window. Fargo limped over and closed it, then returned to the bed. An hour later, the sun lowered over the horizon. Wide awake and staring at the ceiling, Fargo realized he was having the first symptoms of a severe case of cabin fever. He wanted off this bed, out of this room. Most of all, he wanted out of Tucson. Restless, he got off the bed and pulled the straightback to face the window, then sat and looked out into the night. Boss was out there somewhere, running scotfree. And he could do nothing to stop him. At the thought, Fargo's gun hand clenched into a fist.

Bootsteps approaching his door broke Fargo's thoughts about Boss. He looked over his shoulder and waited and watched the doorknob. He heard the three crisp knocks, then McCord's voice say, "Fargo, are you up and receiving?"

"Yeah, Pinky. Come on in."

McCord entered, holding a bottle of bourbon. "Compliments of Mitchell," he said. He handed Fargo the bottle. "Mitch says you can have all of the stuff you want. I asked him if I got plugged would he make me the same offer."

"What did he answer?"

"Didn't, unless you call a laugh an answer. Are you going nuts, yet?"

Fargo pulled the cork. "A little. How did you pass time while confined?"

McCord chuckled. "Slept most of the time. When awake, I thought about how I would break out. And promised myself that I would die before I let the law do this to me again."

"So, the confinement got to you." Fargo took a hit from the bottle, then handed it to Pinky.

Pinky took a pull from it before he answered, "Sure did. I came to hate lawmen as much as I respected the sons of bitches."

"When did you decide to become a hired gunman?"

Pinky rested his butt on the window sill, crossed his legs, then began, "In St. Louis. I had a money fight. High stakes. I never saw so much money as that bet on one fight. And practically all of it was bet against me. The guy who promoted the fight made a ring out of cotton bales. About a hundred men, mostly bankers and their kind, all of them greedy men, fenced around those bales to watch me have the shit whipped out of me. Well, they figured wrong. Oh, I took a beating all right. The other guy broke my nose, split both lips, loosened my teeth, broke my jaw and two ribs, closed one of my eyes, and raised a bunch of knots on my head before my uppercut stunned him. Then he was all mine. Smelling blood, I went to work on him. They said I pounded him with so many hard blows they lost count. Finally he fell. I was sore for a week. For that fight, I got twenty dollars, and the loser, five. Small consolation for beating up one another.

"Later, the promoter came to my room. He told me there was a way to make money without getting hurt. He asked if I knew how to shoot. I told him no, that I didn't carry a gun. He gave me one and offered me a hundred dollars to kill a wealthy man. So, he hired me and my gun. I shot the man in the heart. Later, I learned the promoter and the man's wife had been screwing. The bitch promised him a bucketful of money to get rid of her husband. I got a measly hundred for doing the dirty work.

"I puked after I shot her husband, then again when I learned how much money the promoter got. But the die was cast. What the promoter said was true. I could make a whole lot of money from making my gun available for hire. Anyone with the money could hire it."

"Would you kill a person who you knew? A friend?"

McCord nodded. He took another drink from the bottle, passed it to Fargo, then said, "The new sheriff took four men south to look for the man that got away."

Fargo glanced to sand blasting the windowpane. "He'll find it impossible to track in this sandstorm."

"Yeah, I agree. Ballas is a hard-headed man, though. Maybe he will succeed."

"Did he ask you, Mulllins, and Bassett to ride with him?"

McCord chuckled. "Kid knew he couldn't pay our freight. No, he didn't ask."

"Would you have ridden with a lawman if he hired your gun?"

"Yeah. Law's money folds same as crook's." Pinky pushed away from the window, said, "We'll jaw some more tomorrow. Right now I think I'll see if a poker game started in the saloon after I left to bring a bottle of bourbon to a sick man." He headed toward the door.

As McCord stepped into the hallway, Fargo told him, "Thanks for bringing the bottle. Tell Mitch I owe him a favor."

McCord closed the door. Fargo listened to his footsteps fade away. The only sounds in the room were made from the wind and sand rattling the windowpane. Fargo moved to the bed. Sleep came hard.

* * *

Muted sounds of roosters crowing awakened him at first light. Fargo's bladder was full, and he needed to sit over one of the outhouse holes. Doc said he was to stay in bed. But Doc had forgot about nature calls. Fargo wrapped the sheet around him, then headed for the back stairs.

When he returned, Lillian was bumping her head on his door. Again, her arms were loaded with covered dishes of food. After a head-knock, she called out, "It's me, Lilllian! Rise and shine, Fargo!" She put her right ear to the door.

Barefooted, Fargo came up on her blind side and tapped her shoulder. Lillian jumped back. Fargo caught one dish, she jiggled the other two before capturing them upright. "Fargo, don't ever do that again," she gasped. "You scared me half to death. What are you doing out here, anyhow?"

He shoved the door open, gestured for her to precede him inside. "Nature called," he said. "What's for breakfast?"

Heading for the table, she answered, "You'll see soon enough."

Fargo lifted the cover on the dish he held. The aromas of butter, syrup, and hotcakes teased his nostrils. He lowered the lid and went to sit on the side of the bed and watched Lillian reveal the rest of her breakfast.

"I couldn't remember how you liked your eggs fixed or how many," the cook began. "So I fixed one every which way I knew how, then threw in two hard boiled ones for good measure. So I'll know next time, how many do you like fixed which way?"

"Uh, three, I reckon. Blindfolded or soft scrambled will do."

"Big man like you? Three? What's blindfolded?"

"I don't want the yolks staring up at me."

"Fargo, you mean bastard." She poured him a cup of coffee, then said she had to get back to the cafe. "George ain't good for nothing 'cept filling coffee cups." Lillian went to the window and opened it. Brushing off sand that had collected on the sill, she commented on the weather. "It's a pretty day, Fargo. Not a cloud in the sky. The air is still, too. But in these parts, when the sun comes up, a breeze comes with it." She stepped away from the window.

He watched her gather last night's dishes. Gripping the coffeepot bail with one finger, she left. Fargo looked at the meat plate; two pork chops, thick sliced bacon, a hunk of fried leftover baked ham, sausage, and leftover roast beef. A bread basket piled high with biscuits sat next to a bowl of butter. He started with the eggs.

The sun was well up by the time he finished. Fargo took the coffeepot, cup, and saucer to the window, set the coffeepot on the floor, the cup and saucer on the sill. He got his Colt, then sat in the straightback and filled the cup. He sipped from the steaming brew while he gave the Colt a good cleaning. It was something to do.

Shortly, he heard people and wagons moving about on Main. Tucson was coming alive. He looked at the saloon. Two men led the butchers' horses in the direction of the livery. He knew they were taking the horses to Charlie's corral next to the livery. The horses, saddles, and tack would be sold. Unk would give Sheriff Ballas the dead men's guns to add to the collection in the desk drawer. "Life goes on," Fargo mumbled.

As he watched, Kid and the posse returned. After talking for a moment, the posse rode away. Kid dismounted and hitched his horse to a hotel rail, then came inside. Fargo met him at the door. "Sit and tell me about it," Fargo said. He gestured to him to take the chair, then moved to the bed.

Kid said, "We didn't find him. The blowing sand completely covered his tracks. However, before it did, we saw he had veered away from Sahuarita, but only slightly.

He obviously did not know about the village, otherwise he would've headed straight to it.''

Fargo nodded.

Kid pulled a much-folded sheet of paper from his hip pocket. Pitching it to Fargo, he explained, ''Unk found it on the man that came through the swinging doors.''

Fargo opened the sheet and saw it was a ''wanted'' poster that read: WANTED DEAD OR ALIVE! PETE MILLER. In smaller letters, it went on to say Pete had killed the sheriff of Fort Worth, Texas, and his deputy. It gave Pete's height—six feet—and weight—two-hundred pounds—and mentioned a scar on the back of his right hand. A sketch of Miller wasn't included. Fort Worth put a $1,000 price on Pete's head. ''They want him real bad to offer that much,'' Fargo muttered.

''The question is, why did the dead man have it in his pocket?''

''Could mean either one of two things. He hoped to run across Pete and collect the reward, or he knew Pete Miller. I suggest the first. He and the others came down from Colorado. That's damn far from Forth Worth. But you never know. He could have known Pete Miller. What do you think?''

''Don't rightly know. Anyhow, you keep it. The next time you see McCord, show it to him. He wouldn't tell me anything, but he would you, if he knows or has heard about Miller.''

Fargo nodded. He folded and tucked the poster under his pillow.

Kid said, ''You remember the smithy's eldest son, Timothy?''

''Yes, Tim Duke is a fine lad, big like his father, Lloyd. Why?''

"He's grown since you last saw him. Tim rode in the posse. Coming back, I offered him my deputy badge, and he accepted it."

"Good choice, Kid. Tim will make a good deputy. He's all law and order, just like Lloyd."

Kid stood and went to the door, where he paused to say, "I'm going home and go to bed. *Hasta luego, amigo.* Don't forget to show the poster to McCord."

Fargo nodded. The door closed behind Kid Ballas.

Fargo alternated sitting at the window and lying on the bed. Lillian brought dinner and took away the breakfast dishes. Mid-afternoon found him sitting at the window watching comings and goings on the street below. He heard a soft rap on the door, one that he didn't recognize, and wondered who it might be. Covering himself from the waist down with the sheet, he said, "Come on in."

The Gibbons woman opened the door and stepped just inside. She glanced around the room, then said, "I'm not disturbing you, am I?"

"Not in the least. Pardon my bad housekeeping. I don't get around too good. Please, don't stand there and have to raise your voice. Come stand at the window while we chat."

Mildred stepped to the wall beside the window. Fidgeting with her fingers, she offered an apology. "I fear it was my fault you got shot. I—"

Fargo cut her off. "No need to take the blame, ma'am. I simply wasn't fast enough. Earlier wounds in my left shoulder caused my slowness. They're to blame, not you."

Mildred sighed, relieved and relaxed, then explained, "I'm from Kentucky. Louisville. I taught at one of the schools there."

When she paused, Fargo wondered what she was leading up to.

"My name is—"

"Mildred Gibbons," Fargo interrupted.

She visibly tensed. "Oh, how did you know? What else do you know about me, if you don't mind my asking?"

"Nothing. Sheriff Ballas told me your name. Do you know mine?"

Mildred blushed as she answered, "I asked Mr. Schmidt your name and room number. I'm in number two on the ground floor. Your name is Skye Fargo."

She paused again. Fargo inquired, "What brought you to Tucson, ma'am?"

"Please, Mr. Fargo, call me Mildred, or Millie. I read a notice in the Louisville newspaper that said, in so many words, the marriage agency would find me a man to marry out here on the frontier. They matched me up with a man from Colorado, who would meet me in Tucson. I was to take the Butterfield Stage in time to arrive on the appointed date. And I did. He didn't meet me. Neither is he registered in the hotel. Now I'm in a quandry as to what to do." She sighed heavily.

From Colorado, Fargo thought, then asked, "What is the man's name?"

She answered easily enough, "Otis Earl Puckett."

"Well, Mildred, you saw him."

"Oh? Why didn't he meet me?"

"Because Otis Earl got his head blown off by a double-barrel shotgun blast."

Her knees buckled, and Mildred slid down the wall, gasping, "Oh, my goodness. The poor man."

Fargo saw tears well up in her eyes, her chin pinch and tremble. He said, "No need to fret, Mildred. Raymond's shotgun saved you from committing a deadly mistake. Otis Earl was one of the five men I shot it out with. He put the bullet hole in my thigh. Those five men left a trail of blood, rape, and thievery between here and Colorado."

Mildred Gibbons fainted.

Fargo picked her up and laid her on the bed. He fanned her face with the empty meat dish. Mildred's eyes fluttered open. She mumbled, "Oh, my word. What is the world coming to? I paid the agency one hundred dollars for a rapist."

"You pay your money, you take your chances. Like I said, you were lucky this time."

He failed to notice the sheet had fallen off while he carried her to the bed. Mildred did not. Her widened eyes stared at his organ only inches away from her face. When she gulped, Fargo looked down and saw he stood naked. He spun around to retrieve the sheet. The leg gave way, he stumbled and fell to the floor. Mildred shot off the bed and came to help him get up and lie on the bed. Fargo drew the sheet up. Only then did her gaze move to his face.

She gulped, "Oh, dear me, I must be going. Do you mind if I look in on you again, tomorrow?"

"Certainly you can. Anytime. It will break my otherwise boredom. Sorry that Otis Earl didn't work out for you."

Backing to the door, Mildred replied, "All things come out as they should. Have a good day, Mr. Fargo. May I call you Skye?"

"Of course." He wondered what she meant when referring to things.

Mildred cracked a smile, slipped through the doorway and quietly closed the door.

An hour after the schoolmarm left, Doc walked in unannounced. "How's the thigh today, Fargo?"

"Mite sore."

"Let's have a look at it." Doc pulled the sheet down. "You've been on your feet. It won't crust over if you don't obey my orders."

"I had to go to the outhouse," Fargo mumbled.

"Oh, did you now?" Doc nodded toward the slop jar on the floor across the table. "What's wrong with using that?"

"Dammit, Doc, there's no one to empty it, and I don't want to stink up the room."

"Hunh!" Doc snorted. "I'll tell Gus to come check once every hour when he is awake."

"What about night calls, huh, Doc?"

"You can use the jar or hold it in till morning. I mean it, Fargo. I don't want you getting out of bed. It's for your own good." He opened his medical bag.

Fargo watched and felt him clean the two holes, then spread the salve around them. Doc said, "Sit up, so I can check the back of your shoulder."

Fargo rose into a sitting position, saying, "Those hurt spots feel tight as hell."

"Wouldn't be surprised. They're healing. Scabbing over. That causes the tightness you feel. They're all right. Fresh air is the best thing for them. Try sleeping on your stomach as much as you can." He closed the bag, then stood to say, "Got to get back to the office. Mrs. Bullard is bringing Wilma in for the tonsilectomy. I'll need to visit the saloon for damn sure after that. You stay off your feet, Fargo. I mean it."

Fargo said nothing as he watched the door close behind Doc McPherson. He waited until he heard Doc's footsteps move down the hall to the stairs, then got up and sat in the chair.

An hour later, Gus entered without knocking. "Hate to barge in on you this way, Fargo, but Chance ordered me to—"

Fargo interrupted, "Doc's always handing out orders. He would make a great general. I haven't used the slop jar."

"I can see that."

"I won't, either. I'll go out back."

"Chance said—"

"I know what he said."

"But, but, but—"

"Get out of here, Gus. *Vamoose!*"

Mumbling to himself, shaking his head, Gus left.

Lillian brought his supper, then returned to the cafe. Evening shadows stretched across Main. Fargo watched those creeping from the window sill leave a stark, constrasting pattern of black and white on the floor. Finally, he lit the lamp. And pissed in the slop jar. It was like Doc to come check the damn thing on his way home from the saloon, Fargo reminded himself.

No sooner thought than he heard footsteps in the hall. "McCord," he muttered. When the footsteps stopped at his door, Fargo called out, "Come on in, Pinky."

Pinky entered and shut the door. Fargo saw he gripped a bottle by its neck. Pinky came and sat on the floor and leaned his back against the sill to face Fargo sitting in the chair. Grinning, Pinky handed him the bottle. "Shit, Pinky, the last one is still half full."

"Well, you can always use it to take a bourbon spit bath." He chuckled at his own funny. "Gone insane yet?"

Now Fargo chuckled. "People parade in and out of here so much that I don't have time to go crazy. What's happening in the saloon?"

"Same old six and eight. I'm thinking I might move on. Whip, too."

"Where to?"

"Don't rightly know. One thing's for damn sure. No business around here. Bassett and I are talking about trying Albuquerque."

"There's a folded sheet of paper under my pillow. Fetch it for me, please."

Pinky rose, went and got it. He handed it to Fargo, then

sat again. Fargo unfolded and held the poster to lamplight to see if he could read it. "Take a look at this," he said, and handed it to Pinky.

Pinky twisted and held the poster to the light. Fargo watched McCord's eyes move across and down the poster. Glancing up to Fargo, he lowered the poster and said, "So?"

"You know anything about him?"

"No, Never heard of the man. I've never been in Texas. Where did you come by it?" McCord passed the poster back to Fargo.

"Unk Taylor found it on the man who came at me through the double-doors."

"So?"

Fargo recapped his earlier conversation with Kid about the "wanted."

McCord suggested Bassett might know something about Pete Miller, and went to get him. They returned shortly. Fargo gave Bassett the poster. He took it to the lamp to read it. "Yeah, I know Pete," Bassett said. He came and squatted next to Pinky. Handing the poster to Fargo, he asked, "What do you want to know about Pete?"

McCord explained how Fargo came to possess the poster.

Fargo picked up on it from there. "Sheriff Ballas and I discussed the possibility that the man I shot coming at me from the saloon front doors might have had special interest in Miller. Not necessarily the reward. Anything you can tell me about Pete will help me draw a conclusion."

Bassett began, "While I've only met Pete, I do know he's the oldest of five kids raised by Lester and Irene Miller. Pete has a brother named after his father—Pete called him Junior—and three sisters. Pete told me they had a farm near Weatherford, Texas.

"Pete's a tough man. Mean as hell. He got the scar during a knife fight with an Arab in the Four Jacks Saloon in

Cowtown, over an argument about a French whore that worked in Sadie Nelson's Primrose Path next door. A shapely blonde that posed as a nun.''

"Sister Andre. I know her. Go on."

"Pete killed the Arab and took his funny-looking dagger for a keepsake. It was self-defense, so nothing happened to Pete. It was Pete's word against a dead foreigner's. You know how that goes.

"You reckon it was Junior that you shot?"

Grim-jawed, Fargo nodded. "And Boss is none other than his father, Lester Miller."

6

During the next five days, Doc continued to look in on Fargo every day. So did Kid and McCord and the spinster schoolmarm. Lillian came and went in great regularity. So did Gus. Fargo cleaned his already immaculate Colt and Arkansas-toothpick at least ten times to relieve his boredom. Doc had insisted he stay in bed for the full seven days. "Next Sunday, Fargo . . . maybe," Doc had said. The bullet holes scabbed over. Fargo began exercising almost constantly. Situps and pushups, mostly.

Saturday afternoon Doc walked in without knocking and saw Fargo doing situps. All of his regular visitors no longer bothered to knock. Because Fargo sweated profusely, Doc knew he had been exercising quite a long time this day. Doc sat to wait for him to call it quits.

Finally Fargo mumbled, "Two hundred," and fell backward onto the floor. He shot Doc a wink, then started leg raises.

Doc watched Fargo's abdominal muscles tighten rock-hard a few times before asking, "How long has this exercising been going on?"

Fargo grunted, "Since day two. I was bored. I was getting fat from Lillian's food."

"Do you have any pain?"

"A little," Fargo admitted. Doc didn't need to know the

leg raises especially hurt like hell. "At first," he added. "Once I get started, I loosen up and it goes away."

Doc watched him raise his stiffened legs about a foot off the floor, then start parting and bringing them back together slowly. "Ye Gods, Fargo, you're murdering yourself. Can't fool me. I know that hurts like shit. Stop, I've seen enough."

"Two more, Doc, and I'm through."

Doc reached for the five partially filled bottles of amber liquid lined up next to the wall below the window. Choosing one, he brought it to his mouth and took a swig. Making a face, he said, "I don't know how you drink this poison." He took another swig.

Fargo stood and started wiping sweat off his body with a towel. He asked, "Doc, are you going to let me out of this cage tomorrow?"

"Don't see why not. You would dress and leave, anyhow. I won't be back. Drop by my office Monday morning to let me take a final look at your wounds. I'm more concerned about your left shoulder than your thigh. Sonny boy, in spite of your ability to exercise, you're far from being healed. And you know it."

"Yeah, Doc, I know it. I won't be fit till I can twist violently and run like a scared antelope without any hurting."

"A week to ten days ought to put you in the condition to do it." He rose and headed for the door, where he paused to remind, "Monday morning?"

"I'll be there," Fargo assured him.

Doc started to close the door, then left it open when he walked away. Fargo knew why when he heard Kid's footfalls in the hall. Kid came inside smiling. He said, "Doc had a glum expression on his puss and was shaking his head when we passed. What's up?"

Fargo chuckled. "He caught me doing situps."

"What's the verdict? Is he going to release you tomorrow?"

Fargo nodded.

"I know you are happy for that. What next, Mr. Fargo?" Kid moved to the chair and sat.

From the bed, Fargo answered, "Lester Miller. I know he's out there somewhere within a hundred and fifty mile or so radius. That circle will expand by the time I go after him. First, I have to get back my running strength. While Miller's tracks are ice-cold, I will find him. The man has my Sharps. I intend to get it back."

Kid suggested, "Miller could be in Mexico by now."

"No problem, Kid. I know my way around in Mexico. I'll catch up to him."

Kid changed the subject. "Mrs. Beauchamp asked me to invite you to dinner tomorrow after church. She's fixing turkey and dressing. Will you come?"

"Of course, I want to meet Miss Katie, anyhow."

That pleased Kid. Blushing, he sighed, then said, "I like her a lot, Mr. Fargo. Miss Katie is so sweet, so innocent."

"Are you thinking about asking her father for her hand in marriage?"

Kid nodded.

"Have you asked her?"

"Yes. Last night in the front porch swing."

"And?" Fargo raised his eyebrows.

"Miss Katie kissed me on the mouth."

"Sounds serious."

Kid stood and leaned out the window. Looking up and down Main, he said, "Gotta go, Mr. Fargo. I see cowhands on lower Main, heading for the saloon. It's going to be a rowdy night." He pulled back and walked to the door.

Fargo threw him a lazy two-finger salute as Kid passed the bed.

Lillian came and went for the last time. Fargo told her he would have breakfast at the cafe tomorrow. Lillian seemed sad that she wouldn't be bringing his meals to the room anymore.

After eating, Fargo sat in the chair and watched the saloon and listened to the cowhands laughing inside until midnight. At that hour, McCord came outside. Looking up, he saw Fargo sitting at the window and aimed yet another bottle of bourbon at him. As he watched Pinky saunter across the intersection, Fargo grinned and shook his head. A few moments later Pinky walked into the room. He sat on the floor under the window.

Fargo asked, "You get all those cowpunchers' money?"

"Naw, they're flat broke. Said they haven't got paid yet. McPherson said you're getting out tomorrow."

"I'm having breakfast at the Clarke's cafe. You want to join me? I'm buying."

Pinky shook his head. "You going after Miller?"

"Soon as I get limbered up."

"Want to hire my gun? Bucky's and Whip's? The four of us can bring a fast end to his life."

"No, Pinky. This is something I have to do alone. Just me and him. I'll let Miller pull iron first, then I'll have the pleasure of sending the bastard to hell."

McCord shifted weight to the other cheek, shook his head. "That's not so smart, Fargo. The man has a charmed life. He might kill you."

"He's already had three chances and failed. Reckon I'm the one who is charmed."

"Mebbe you're right."

They sat a spell longer, nipping on the bourbon, being quiet. Finally McCord stood and said, "By the way, Whip mentioned something about Pete Miller that wasn't on the wanted. Bank robbery. Whip says Pete is flushed with money. Just thought you'd want to know.''

Fargo could care less about Pete Miller. Nonetheless, he nodded.

Pinky said he would see him tomorrow, then he left. Fargo lay down on the bed. He fell asleep visualizing the lay of the land south of Tucson.

Three hours later, the latching mechanism of the door clicked and Fargo opened his eyes. His gun hand slipped beneath the pillow, grasped the Colt. From the glow cast by the lamp, he watched the doorknob turn slowly. Soundlessly, the door eased open. Mildred Gibbons stood there dressed in a white nightgown only. Her widened eyes showed no fear. She had let her hair down and arranged it so the right half tumbled down her back and the other half hung down the left side of her chest. She had opened the top button of her gown. That was exceedingly bold of the spinster, Fargo thought. He eased the hammer down.

Keeping her eyes fixed on his, Mildred slipped inside, shut the door, and leaned against it, her hands at her sides. Fargo propped on one elbow and waited. Finally, her right hand moved slowly to the second button. After a pause, she undid it, then moved her fingers down to the next button, where she paused again.

She's scared to death, Fargo told himself. An innocent fawn facing a cougar for the first time. One slight movement on his part and the fawn would flee. He briefly considered making one, but discarded that thought. Without realizing it, Mildred Gibbons aroused him with the slowly executed, provocative fumbling open of the buttons. Fargo caught himself wanting to see more of the shapely female.

He watched her continue the slow undoing of all the buttons. Her left hand held the nightgown from opening as her right hand fingers worked the last button free. After a long pause that excited Fargo, she released her grip on the front of the gown. It parted by six inches to reveal her nice cleavage and about half of her milk-white breasts, a flat belly having an indented navel, and a thin, narrow patch of dark-brown pubic hair.

He glanced up in time to see her Adam's apple bob once as she silently gulped. She turned her back to him. Looking over her right shoulder at him, she slipped the gown off her shoulders and let it fall to her ankles. Fargo saw an inverted heart-shaped rear end, perfect in all respects. She stepped out of the gown piled around her feet, then bent at the waist to pick it up. For a fleeting moment, she presented Fargo a view of her lower charms, which glistened from her juices. As she turned to face him, she brought the gown to dangle from her cleavage. Twin milk-white breasts the size of firm grapefruits, each having soft-brown areola the size of two-bit pieces, presented her erect pinkish-brown nipples.

Mildred approached his bed slowly, watched his eyes for approval of what they saw. Standing at the bed, she spread her gown and covered his head with it. Fargo caught a whiff of the lilac-scented powder emanating from the gown. His hands went to her buttocks and pulled her into the bed. Mildred removed the gown from his face and gazed into his lake-blue eyes.

Grasping his throbbing manhood, she whispered, "Take me, big man. Please?"

Not that it mattered—after all she had come to him voluntarily—but he asked, anyhow, "Mildred, are you a virgin?"

"No. When I was fourteen, a sixteen-year-old and I were playing on a haystack, and he—well, you know. That was the first and only time for me, and the first for him. It was sort of clumsy, but he managed to break my maidenhead.

When he saw the blood, Frank fainted. We didn't try again."

Fargo fondled her breasts, then slid his right hand down over her belly and dipped the middle finger into her juicy slit. She arched her back and raised her hips, moaned, "Oh, yes, yes, yes . . . that's what I've waited so long to feel. More. Don't stop . . . please, don't stop." Her breathing quickened.

Fargo parted the blood-swollen lips and worked the finger into the tight opening. Circling it to make her juices flow even more and lubricate the tight tunnel, he whispered, "Are you sure you want to do this? It's going to hurt at first."

She whimpered, "I don't care. Yes, oh, yes, I want to feel you inside me." Mildred raised her hips a tad higher and began to sway them slowly.

Keeping the finger in, Fargo kissed both her supple breasts. Her fingers entwined in his hair and held his face tightly to her bosom. She mewed, "Frank didn't do that. It feels so good. I'm getting dizzy, big man. So light-headed."

Fargo nursed on her left breast while his finger glided in and out of her moist, hot sheath, and rubbed hard on the top of the slit. She moaned her joy, "Oh, my God . . . oh, my God, I've never . . . felt this good before. Suck the other one, too. Oh, yes . . . please, suck it hard." She twisted her right breast to his lips.

Fargo rolled the nipple between his teeth, then took in as much of the breast as his mouth would hold. Mildred gasped, "I'm in heaven." One of her hands went to his at her crotch and encouraged him to probe deeper.

Fargo rolled atop her and parted her slender legs with his knees. When she started gulping, he kissed her open mouth. Her hot tongue caressed his and she whimpered in his mouth, "Oh, Jesus, I'm on fire. Give it to me. Hurry, please."

Fargo nodded. Then he raised his left knee and put it between her legs at the knees and pressed outward on her right leg. Mildred got the idea. She moved the leg out as far as she could. Fargo raised the other knee, and she quickly spread her legs to let him be on his knees between them. Fargo put his hands under her knees and lifted her hips until the head of his manhood parted her hot lips and touched the soft, tender opening, ready for entry.

Mildred lay submissive, arms outstretched, legs limp, body relaxed, smiling. Her widened eyes conveyed a mixture of joyous anticipation, awe that it was really happening to her, and fear of the great unknown. Mildred held her breath and nodded.

Fargo raised her knees a tad higher and felt his sensitive, blood-swollen crown penetrate the slick entrance. Her reaction was instantaneous. Her thighs tightened, and he felt her heels brush his buttocks. Mildred's body stiffened as she gasped between clinched teeth, "Aaagh!"

Fargo slowly inserted half his length. Her eyes flared, then shut tightly. Spittle seeped from the corners of her tightened lips. She began squirming, raised her hips higher and higher. Fargo knew he was in where no man had been before. Slippery though her love-tunnel was, it was still the tightest he had ever been encased by.

Mildred moaned, "Oh, oh, you're so big, so big, and hard." Her hands came to his chest. She dug her fingernails into his pectoral muscles until blood appeared. The sight of blood oozing from around her fingernails excited Mildred into a frenzy. Without warning, she commenced bucking furiously, driving him in deeper and deeper. Her heels dug into his buttocks and coaxed him to give her more. Her head tossed and she screamed her joy, "Oh, God! More, more! Harder! Faster! Yes, yes, go faster! Aaaeeyii!" She bent at the waist and embraced him tightly, her fingernails now raking his back, and her moist lips kissing all over his chest, throat, and face.

Fargo felt her several orgasms grip him. He moved his hands to her buttock cheeks and pulled and fused her wild-moving hot opening to the base of his length.

He helped maximize her pleasure by rolling his hips in the opposite direction to expand the slippery opening. Mildred clawed his back and moaned, "This is so wonderful. I've never felt this way." She raised and pressed her left breast to his lips, entwined her fingers in his hair.

Fargo sucked in a mouthful of the breast. She gasped, "Oh, oh, yes, yes, yes, so good, that's it . . . that's it!"

Fargo felt her powerful contraction seize around his full length and start milking. She was whimpering now, her head lolling, clutching him tightly to her breast, whispering, whimpering, "Jesus, what's happening to me down there?"

The milking triggered his eruption. She screamed for joy, "Oh, my God! Oh, my God! Flood me, big man, oh, yes, flood me!" Then her body fell limp. Her hands dropped from his head, her feet moved off his buttock cheeks, and Mildred collapsed backward onto the bed.

Licking her lips, the little hellcat murmured, "I love you big man. I'll never be the same again, because of you. I'm so happy."

Fargo had heard it before. Many times. He pulled her to him and nestled her head in the crook of his good shoulder. She sighed, then drew tiny circles with her fingers on his left breast as they drifted into a peaceful sleep.

As roosters crowed that the sun was up, Fargo got out of bed and dressed, then went outside. Mildred Gibbons had sapped him dry. He headed for the Clarkes' cafe. George saw him coming and had a steaming cup of freshly brewed coffee waiting when Fargo opened the door.

George grinned and said, "Fargo, you look like you have been in a cat fight and lost. Sit before you fall down." He shoved the cup and saucer across the counter to Fargo, then shouted over his shoulder to Lillian in the kitchen, ''Four eggs sunny-side up with a thick slice of ham and a half-dozen hot biscuits!''

Lillian called back, ''That you, Skye Fargo?''

Fargo mumbled, ''Uh, huh. What's left of me.''

''What did you say?'' Lillian yelled.

George answered, ''Better hurry, honey. He's dying.''

Lillian poked her head through the doorway to see for herself, then gasped, ''Fargo, go to your room and get back in the bed! You look like hell. I'll bring food to you.''

Fargo groaned. He wasn't about to tangle with the school-marm hellcat again. Not today at least. Actually, he hoped she would take his teachings elsewhere, try them out with another man. Fargo muttered, ''Fix six eggs, Lillian. Quick.'' He raised the cup to his lips and took a sip. Then he looked at George and mumbled, ''George, never teach a teacher a new subject. Not unless you have plenty of running room.''

George Clarke frowned. ''Lillian has been telling me your appetite is good, your color looks good, your humor's good—nothing but good, according to her.''

''Well, George, I think I had a mild relapse,'' Fargo lied. The Clarkes didn't need to know everything. Fargo quickly changed the subject. ''It's going to be a hot day.''

''A scorcher for this late in the year. Wouldn't be surprised to see it cloud up and rain.''

So they talked about the weather until Lillian appeared with his breakfast. Lillian's sunnyside-ups vanished right in front of her batting eyes.

Fargo buttered four biscuits. Raymond and Sam Hutchinson walked in as he was sopping red-eye gravy with half of one. They sat on either side of him. After telling George what they wanted in the way of breakfast, Raymond said, "Fargo, you look like something the cat dragged in."

George replied, "He ain't telling. I've already tried and he got off on the weather."

Fargo managed a weak grin. He kept on sopping red-eye and finishing off the slab of ham. Sam was still so sleepy that for him to engage in conversation was out of the question. Ray didn't talk about the weather, but he did change the subject. "Last night Doc told me that he found you exercising down on the floor."

"What I need is a real bath," Fargo said. "Bucket baths are lacking."

Sam said, "Mebbe I can talk Ira into unlocking the barber-shop long enough for you to use one of his tubs."

"Fine idea," Fargo began. "I'm due at the Beauchamps for Sunday dinner. Before that, I'm going to run a little to strengthen my legs. I'll need a tub bath after running."

"I'll go ask Ira for the key when I leave here," Sam said. Fargo nodded.

Pinky, then Bucky came in and took stools at the counter. George told them about Fargo's intention to run and have a bath at Ira Kane's barbershop. Bucky suggested, "I'll be glad to heat the water for a free bath."

"I'll mention your offer to Ira," Sam replied.

Pinky said, "Ira's got five tubs. I won thirty dollars off Cutler last night. Why don't I make it right by Ira and pay him to let us use four. Me and Fargo, Bucky, and Whip. I'll give Ira five dollars of Cutler's money to let us soak as long as we want."

Sam chuckled. "He'll jump at the offer."

The morning crowd at Clarke's cafe adjourned to Mitchell's saloon, where they sat to watch Raymond sweep the floor and clean last night's glasses while waiting for Fargo to get in the mood to run and for the barbershop key to arrive.

Finally, Fargo eased out of his chair and said, "I'm ready to run."

"Where?" Bucky asked.

Fargo was halfway to the swinging doors before he made up his mind and answered, "Up and down Main is as good a place as any."

Everyone followed him as far as the porch. They sat in the shade and dangled their feet off the edge of the porch and sipped from bottles of whiskey while they watched the big man strip to the waist. He draped his shirt, gun belt, and calf-sheath over a hitching rail, put his boots and socks, hat and neckerchief below it, then did a few knee-bends to limber up.

Whip said, "Fine looking Arkansas-toothpick and calf-sheath you have there, Fargo. Wouldn't want to sell them, would you?"

Fargo shook his head. "No, Whip. Just like my horse and everything else I have, none are for sale or trade." He did a final deep knee-bend, then jogged away, up Main.

At the livery, he turned and jogged back past them to Unk Taylor's funeral parlor on lower Main, where he paused to catch his wind. He looked at his pant's leg where the bullet had entered and saw no bloodstain. The thigh was still tight, but other than that it felt sound to him. He quickened his pace on the return trip. Passing the watchers, they whistled and clapped. Pinky yelled, "Fargo, I'm glad it's you and not me! Getting in shape for a fight is a pain in the ass!"

Fargo didn't slow down as he used the full width of the street to turn at the livery and come back down Main. Approaching the intersection, he saw Mildred standing at the window, fumbling with the buttons on her gown. She blew him a kiss, then smiled winsomely.

Pinky and the others had seen her, too. When he ran past

them, they blew him kisses and batted their eyes, and made little love sounds. Now they knew, Fargo thought.

At Unk's he picked up speed. Sweat poured from his body by the time he turned at the livery and added even more speed. Fargo made a wide swing at Unk's place, then ran as hard and fast as his legs and feet could back to the saloon. Gasping for air, he braced on the hitching rail.

Fargo carried his clothing to the barbershop. When Sam unlocked the door, the gunslingers took off their hats and neckerchiefs. Sam pushed the door open. They filed through the barbershop to the bath area out back. Five wooden tubs surrounded the fire heating the huge cast-iron kettle of water. Sam had it already boiling hot. The area was enclosed by four-foot upright wooden fencing that had plenty of gaps between the planks, numerous cracks and knot holes. A flat roof rested on eight-foot tall poles. A bench stood next to each tub, as did steps for entering them.

Fargo filled his tub with hot and cold water until the temperature felt right for him. The gunslingers did likewise. Then they and Fargo undressed and got in their tubs. Fargo groaned as he sunk chin-deep into the water. He drifted into sleep, listening to the others chat back and forth.

The falling water temperature awakened him. He saw the hour was about eleven o'clock, and the gunslingers were asleep in their tubs. Fargo scrubbed the filth off his body, got out of the tub, and toweled dry. He dressed hurriedly, then left without waking them. He arrived at the Beauchamps' home before they or Kid Ballas got there from church services. Fargo sat in the swing to wait. Elly Beauchamp, Katie, and Roy caught Fargo napping. He nearly fell from the swing, coming to his feet. Removing his hat, he mumbled, "Evening, ma'am. You too, Miss Katie."

"Lord's sake, Mr. Fargo, why didn't you go inside and

sit on my couch," Elly admonished. "That old swing is hard."

Kid stepped around her and opened the screen door. "Been here, long, Mr. Fargo?" he asked. The females entered.

Fargo muttered, "Just got here." He gestured for Kid to precede him into the house.

Katie and her mother had disappeared into the kitchen. Fargo heard them chatting about Silas' sermon while setting the table. He and Kid sat to wait. Kid said, "Mr. Beauchamp will be along shortly. He's still shaking people's hands. Mrs. Elly and Katie put the chicken and dressing in to bake just before leaving for church. What did you do all morning?"

Fargo recalled the part about his running only. The preacher came inside just as Fargo concluded, and caught the tail-end. Silas said, "Mr. Hutchinson came and got Ira Kane's key from him. Said you and those gunmen were going to bathe after your run."

"Yes," Fargo verified.

"Roy, you ought to run those devils out of Tucson," Silas suggested. "Those no-goods are up to something evil."

To change the subject, Kid said, "Have you met Miss Mildred Gibbons? Some of us were talking about her at church this morning. Might she be our new schoolmarm?"

Silas took it from there. "Betsy Wardlaw is going back to Joplin, where she was born and raised. Great loss. Great loss."

Kid explained, "Miss Betsy is the schoolmarm."

"Ugly as sin," Silas butted in. "But a good woman. Mighty fine woman. Pure as the driven snow."

Kid went on, "The citizens feel as though their school-marm must be pure if she isn't married. Miss Betsy is leaving next month."

Fargo said nothing. Miss Betsy's and Mildred Gibbons' private lives were just that. As far as he was concerned, they were free to do anything they damn well pleased. While he admired good morals, Fargo knew they were impossible to maintain. One did the best they could and hoped it was good enough for most folks. It had been Fargo's experience that folks who acted self-righteous and spoke against sin—and to their way of thinking sin meant sex—were the first to sneak around and do the exact opposite. Kid Ballas was a good and decent man. However, Kid had his flaws, too, like any man. Kid needed to leave this house at the earliest possible opportunity, else he would begin to mimic Silas' self-righteous attitudes. Silas had branded Miss Betsy ugly as sin. To Fargo's way of thinking, ugly was relative. Compared to what? Silas had suggested Kid should run the gunslingers out of town, they were up to something evil. That, too, was a relative word. Evil as compared to what? Silas was being judgmental about the morals of others, and Fargo didn't like that. Silas wasn't perfect.

Fargo heard them speaking, but didn't listen. His mind was on other matters, like moving on. He had seen enough of Tucson. Coming here had brought him nothing but grief. On the other hand, he asked himself, might not have God put him in the path of the butchers for a good reason? Yes, he told himself. God kept me alive on purpose. He intends for me to send Lester Miller, the last of the butchers, to heaven or hell.

Katie's voice broke into his thoughts. "Dinner is on the table," she announced from the kitchen doorway.

As a unit, the men stood and went into the kitchen. The aroma of baked chicken, dressing, and all the trimmings of a grand Sunday dinner teased Fargo's nostrils and made his mouth water. Elly gestured for him to sit across from her at one end of the table. Silas sat at the head of the table, Katie next to her mother, and Kid next to Fargo.

Fargo studied Katie while Silas said grace. Kid had said

Katie was sixteen. She looked a tad younger. Fargo wondered if her father considered her pretty face as being ugly? Katie had soft-brown hair and eyes, a supple figure on the fleshy side, and stood, he reckoned, about five-two. Kid had picked a winner.

Silas muttered, "Amen."

While starting bowls and platters of food around the table, Elly became Fargo's chief interrogator. "Now that Dr. McPherson has released you, Mr. Fargo, what are your immediate plans?"

"Get my strength back, ma'am."

"Come now, Mr. Fargo, you know what I meant."

Fargo suddenly realized he was being baited. Why, he didn't know. There was only one way to find out; speak the truth. "No, ma'am, I don't know what you meant. If you care to explain, I'll answer best I can."

Elly put a wing on her husband's plate.

Fargo reckoned she was choosing her words.

"Beans, Mr. Fargo?" She reached for the bowl of butterbeans.

Now he knew she was buying time. Apparently Kid and Katie weren't interested in the discussion. They were too busy being proper young lovers, eye-talking, quick smiles, and all that. Kid blushed twice, and that seemed to amuse Katie. Fargo reckoned their feet were touching under the table.

Silas, however, was keenly aware of Elly's thrust. It showed in his silence and eyes, which prompted her to get on with it. Silas was the type, Fargo decided, who let his wife ask the questions while he pondered the answers, then at the conclusion would make a profound, trapping statement designed to prove wrong the person being questioned.

If it was a game they wanted to play, Fargo concluded, then a game they'd get. He said, "Ma'am, I already have beans on my plate. You were saying?"

"Are you leaving Tucson? Uh, before or after?"

Riddles, Fargo thought. Before or after could mean most anything. "After," he answered.

As though Fargo had understood what Elly meant and committed himself to whatever it was, Elly and Silas smiled wickedly, then she said, "Good, then it's settled." She glanced at her husband and added, "Mr. Fargo accepts."

Silas nodded.

Fargo wondered what he had agreed to.

Elly told him, "If possible, we would prefer you kill them in the saloon. That way it will strengthen our contention that the saloon is an evil place."

Kill who, Fargo thought? This game was getting out of hand.

Silas made his profound statement. Laying down his fork, he looked at Fargo and said, "Rod Mitchell and his saloon is the last bastion of sin in Tucson. He and it collect all the filth. Makes decent folks turn away from the Lord. That harlot who plied her trade in his saloon, and the three ranch hands who were murdered with her are good examples. God wants to put an end to the saloon and those three evil gunmen."

So, Fargo thought, that's it. They expect me to do their dirty work. Well, God didn't whisper anything in my ear. They want me to put my life on the line to save Kid's. He would if—Fargo looked at Kid and asked, "What do you say about it?"

"Er, uh, about what?" Kid answered, frowning.

"Me going up against McCord, Mullins, and Bassett. Elly and Silas have proposed I do it."

A shocked expression registered on Kid's face, as Fargo figured it would. Kid didn't blush. His face turned red from anger. He looked down the table at Elly and Silas and said evenly, "I'm the sheriff in Tucson. I will determine who and what is unlawful, not you. The day a majority of our citizens vote to abolish saloons, I will uphold the law, Not before. And as far as those three men are concerned, none have broken any law. Until they do, I will not harass or otherwise bother them.''

"But, but," sputtered Elly, lamely, a hurt look on her face.

Silas came to her rescue. Pounding a fist on the table, he thundered, "Young man, I determine the morality of Tucson! And I say the saloon is a den of iniquity, an evil place where foul men and shameless whores gather! I want—!''

Kid rose from his chair. He trembled with rage, so much so that he gripped the edge of the table to keep from moving down it to the preacher. Kid's eyes were mere slits as he retaliated, "Sir, you have offended me and your guest. My sweet departed wife was a most gentle, generous, and God-fearing woman. She did more for the community at Welsenburg than you even thought about doing for Tucson. Vanessa was a saloonkeeper. All the citizens, men, women, children, and the town's preacher adored her.''

Elly swooned. Silas fell back in his chair and started gagging. Katie froze in shock.

Kid looked at Katie and said, "Miss Katie, will you marry me?''

The young woman glanced at her mother and father. "Mama, Papa?''

"No!" roared Silas. "It's unthinkable to expect me to give Katie's hand in marriage to the likes of you! Get out of my home! Both of you!''

Fargo watched Kid spin and stride out of the kitchen. Then he stood to follow. Facing Katie, he said, "You have just lost a good man.''

Out on the porch, Fargo watched Kid ride away at a gallop. He looked at the swing and shook his head sadly. Honesty had lost it forevermore to Kid.

Three more days of running put him in shape. Kid had

taken a room in the hotel. While Kid acted as though nothing had happened, Fargo knew he was hurting on the inside. He also knew Kid would get over it, in time.

On the morning of the fourth day, Fargo went to Charlie's livery and made the Ovaro ready for the trail. Then he walked the stallion to the saloon and went inside. Raymond was sweeping the floor. He looked up when Fargo came in. "You're going," he said.

"Yes," Fargo replied. "Came by to have a drink and say *adios, amigo.*"

Raymond leaned his broom against the bar, then moved behind it and filled a shot glass with bourbon. Handing it to Fargo, he said, "It's on the house, big man. Where are you headed out for?"

"Reckoned I'd mosey down Sahuarita way and see if he's there."

"Sahuarita, huh?" Raymond echoed.

"Yeah," Fargo muttered. "It's a shot in the dark, I know, but I have to start somewhere. I don't expect to find him there, but you never know. I haven't got anything better to do than track Miller down." He drank his bourbon, then pushed back from the bar and shook hands with Raymond.

A westbound Butterfield stage rumbled around the corner. Fargo glanced through the windows at it, then shot Raymond a wink, and ambled out of the saloon. He strolled to the Ovaro hitched to the rail on Cactus Street.

Mounting up, he saw the stage driver on top of the celerity pass down a saddle to a husky passenger on the ground. The man shoved his black hat back on his head, hefted the saddle onto his shoulder, then headed for the hotel.

Fargo exchanged nods with the fellow, then turned the Ovaro and rode south on Main.

7

The air was deathly still. Faint leather creaks and the plod of the stallion made the only sounds. Four buzzards circled lazily high above Fargo. Dust devils whirled and skipped all around him, most in the distance, a few nearby. He glanced behind. Highly magnified by the shimmering heat waves that rippled off the hot sand, Tucson loomed big as life and made it appear he was entering the town, not six miles away. No ruts left by wagons or hoofprints showed Fargo the way to Sahuarita. He relied on the cruel sun that blazed white-hot in the cloudless milky sky. He faced forward and stared briefly through the heat waves, then pulled his neckerchief up below his eyes.

Shortly after sunset, he rode into the Mexican village. With no adobe walls around the village to protect it, the hovels of Sahuarita caught the drifting sand. Passing between two rows of sod-roofed adobe houses, he saw candle or lamplight spilling through open windows and doorways, heard movement inside, mothers coaxing their young to eat. He halted at a doorway, rapped on the wall and called inside, "*Senora,* does Sahuarita have a cantina?"

The silence beyond the doorway was instantaneous. A chubby woman, carrying an infant on one hip, appeared just inside the doorway and looked up at the Anglo stranger astride the black and white pinto. Fargo touched the brim of his hat and repeated, "I'm looking for the cantina. Do you have one?"

"*Si, senor.*" She stepped outside. Keeping a wary eye on Fargo, she pointed down the corridor. "The cantina is down there. Beyond the well."

Again, Fargo touched the brim of his hat. "*Gracias, senora,*" he said, and nudged the Ovaro forward in a slow walk.

He found the well and cantina easily enough, and halted at the entrance of the latter. He dismounted and ground-reined the stallion, stepped to the entrance, and looked inside the narrow room. An aproned bartender and four men sat at a table, conversing in low tones about a bean field. The bartender noticed Fargo and stiffened. The others fell silent and followed his gaze to the open front door.

Fargo nodded to them and stepped casually to the bar. The bartender hurried behind it. He asked nervously, "Do you want a drink, *senor*? All I have is tequila and a few bottles of *cerveza.*"

"Tequila," replied Fargo. He indicated two fingers deep. While the bartender filled his order, Fargo turned to face the four men and rested the small of his back on the edge of the bar. The men stared at his holstered Colt, as though he might suddenly draw it and shoot all of them. When he heard the bartender slide the glass to him, Fargo reached behind without looking and picked up the glass. He took it and sat in the chair the bartender had vacated. The men's stony expressions conveyed nothing to the big man. He wasn't surprised. They were waiting to learn why he was here.

Fargo sid, "Relax, *senors*. I come in peace. All I want is information and a place to put my horse while I'm in your village."

The bartender spoke, "*Senor*, my name is Hector. Hector

Gonzales. What is this information you want from us? We know nothing. We are only poor peons, *senor*."

Fargo said, "I'm searching for an Anglo. A bad Anglo. His name is Lester Miller. He's a big fellow. Rides a gray dappled mare. We shot and killed four of his men eleven days ago in Tucson. Have any of you seen such a man or his horse?"

Fargo watched them exchange glances. Finally the man sitting across from him answered, "No, *senor*, we haven't seen this Anglo, and we don't want to. You can put your horse in the shed at our goat pen. When do you leave Sahuarita?"

Fargo chuckled inwardly. It was obvious they wanted him out of their village at the earliest possible moment. Trouble begets trouble, he mused, then said, "I leave at dawn."

The man sitting on his left asked, "Where will you sleep, *senor*?"

It sounded as though they wanted him to bed down as far away from the village as possible. Fargo answered, "Oh, I will find a place near my horse." He took a swallow from the glass.

Hector said, "The goat pen? It's at the end of this row of homes, *senor*. Follow your nose."

As a unit, the four men rose. After nodding toward Hector, they left. Hector brought the bottle of tequila and sat across from Fargo. Hector explained, "They have gone to tell the people about you and the bad Anglo you seek."

"It is a wise thing to do, Hector. The Anglo put two bullets in me. And I was armed the second time. Have you heard of a village north of here?"

"*Si, senor*, we know *villa deserto de diablo*. Many of us have relatives there. Why?"

Fargo told him about the butchers riding in at night to rape and slaughter the villagers. Hector quickly crossed himself, then asked, "Who did they murder?"

"I know only two names. Maria and Papa Fuentes."

Hector gasped as he slumped back in his chair. Again, he crossed himself, then asked, "How many others did they kill?"

"I counted eleven bodies at the well when I rode out of *villa deserto.*"

"Madre Dio!" gasped Hector. He fell forward and put his head in his hands. "I will light a candle for each of them," he said.

Fargo then told him about the earlier grisly encounter the Jicarillas had with Miller's butchers.

"They are *loco de cabaza.*" Hector whispered, and shook his head. "I see now why you seek this devil. I wish I could help, but I cannot. Thank God he did not come to Sahuarita."

"He came in this direction after the gunfight in Tucson. The sheriff's posse lost him in a sandstorm."

"Si, si. We had a sandstorm at that time."

"Lucky for you. The sheriff told me Miller drifted off course, but continued to ride south. What is the name of the next village south of Sahuarita?"

"Amado. One long day's ride on a horse from here. Then Nogales on the Mexico border. Do you think this bad man went to Amado?"

"Don't rightly know. But the odds are great that he did. A thirsty man and a thirstier horse go to the nearest water. Does Amado have a well?"

"Si. Nogales, too. I hope he died from thirst before finding Amado, God forgive me."

"Miller is a tough *hombre,* Hector. He found water all right. You can bet he did. If not in Amado, then elsewhere."

Hector stood and said, *"Amigo,* what is your name?"

"Skye Fargo."

"Skye Fargo, I must go and tell the people not to be afraid of you. They need to know the sad news about what happened in *villa deserto de diablo*. Papa was a good friend of mine. Many candles will be lit for him, his daughter, Maria, and the others. Sleep well, *amigo*."

Fargo watched Hector hasten outside, then take off running. He downed the rest of the tequila in his glass, then stood and ambled to his horse. He found the goat pen easy enough and put the Ovaro under the shed. While the pinto nibbled hay and drank from a bucket hanging from a big nail in a post, Fargo removed his saddle, tack, and other stuff. He put all but his bedroll on the low roof of the shed, then crossed the narrow lane and pitched his bedroll onto the sod roof of a hovel. A rickety ladder lay on the ground near the pen. He used it to climb to the roof, then spread his bedroll, undressed and got into it. Listening to the babble of excited voices of villagers, he drifted into sleep.

A rooster crowing from atop a hovel nearby awakened him. The sun had risen halfway over the horizon. Children giggled on the street below. Fargo stretched to peer over the edge of the roof.

A tall, slim young woman astride a burro followed close behind a dozen goats. Two little girls ran alongside her. The woman held a long, slim pole which she used to prod a pair of bleating nannies straggling behind the small herd. Her long, raven-black hair, done up in a single braid, hung down her back and touched the burro's spine. She wore a solid yellow skirt trimmed with a black four-inch flounce. Her loose-fitting black blouse was pulled down to her upper arms, in line with her small bosom. Dark eyes were set wide apart on either side of a narrow nose on her slim face. She had a wide mouth, full lips. Pearl-white, even teeth showed when she smiled at the children. Her sandaled feet almost touched the ground. She wore earrings identical to the pair Fargo had given to Maria. She glanced up at Fargo and frowned.

"Buenos dias, senorita," he called down to her.

She didn't acknowledge his greeting right off. She slipped off the burro and lowered the rails in front of the goat pen, then coaxed them with the shaft to go inside. Putting the rails back in place, she looked at him and said in remarkably good English, "Good morning, *senor*." With one foot on the ground, she sat on the top rail to add, "I've seen you and this pretty horse before."

Now Fargo frowned.

She laughed, then explained, "I helped my cousin, Maria, bathe you."

Fargo vaguely remembered. "Your name is?"

"Tia. Tia Burciaga. But you won't remember me. You were unconscious from the fever. Papa and Maria removed the arrowhead from your shoulder. *Si?*"

Fargo nodded. "Do you live in Sahuarita?"

"No, I'm from Amado. I brought these goats from *villa deserto del diablo* to an aunt and uncle of mine. I leave for Amado in the morning." Tia stood and stepped into the middle of the lane and asked, "Are you hungry? Get some clothes on and I'll take you to my aunt's house. Aunt Alicia always has plenty of food."

"Be with you in a minute." Fargo retreated to his clothes and put them on, then rolled and tied his bedding. He dropped the bedroll to the ground, then lowered himself to it. Tia waited for him to put the bedroll on his saddle, then gestured toward the cantina.

Walking to her aunt's, Tia flashed a smile at him and said, "Maria was afraid you would die. We took turns nursing you. Maria had never been so close to an Anglo."

"And you had?"

"*Si*, a few. Damon Finche, mostly. And Damon's cowpuncher friends. He's gone now. So are his friends. Old man Robertson quit ranching."

"Where did you get those earrings?"

Fingering one of them, Tia said, "Off Maria's ears. I prepared her and Papa for burial. The earrings are pretty. Did you give them to her?"

Fargo nodded.

"Do you want them back?"

"No. They look pretty on you."

Pointing to a door, Tia continued, "Aunt Alicia's. Tomas Gomez is her husband. We call him Uncle Tomasita. They have nine little ones. By the way, what is your name, cowboy?"

"Skye Fargo. And, Tia, I'm no cowboy."

She paused at the door, grinned and commented, "If it walks like a duck and quacks like a duck, then it must be a duck. If you aren't a cowboy, what are you?"

"A trailsman."

Tia tossed him a wink, then opened the door.

An older woman stood at the stove. A naked baby nursed her left breast. Eight other children, each a tad taller than the next, sat on both sides of a table with empty plates before them. Everyone looked at Tia and Fargo. Tia spoke in Spanish to her aunt, "*Bueno dias*, Aunt Alicia." Tia moved to stand beside her. "I brought you twelve fat goats."

"I know," Alicia muttered. "Pilar told me they were skinny." Alicia glanced at Fargo standing just inside the doorway. "I heard a big Anglo was here. What are you doing with him?"

"Nothing. Yet. We are hungry. He's a trailsman. I told him you always fixed *mucho* good food."

"Well, for twelve skinny goats, I will feed both of you. Go sit. It's about ready."

Tia gestured for Fargo to sit on the far end of a bench lined with four youngsters. She told them to make room for him, then sat across the table to face Fargo. Tia asked Fargo, "What are you doing in Sahuarita?"

"In Tucson, I shot and killed three of the men that came to *villa deserto del diablo* to murder. A friend shot and killed another one. Their leader escaped, but not before wounding me in the thigh. I'm looking for him."

"Jorge told me one of the rapists shot you in the shoulder back in *villa deserto del diablo* and left you for dead. God must have given you a charmed life, eh, big man?"

"I suppose," Fargo agreed. "Anyhow, the posse said he headed this way. I asked Hector and several men in the cantina if they had seen the man, and they hadn't."

Alicia set plates and flatware in front of Fargo and Tia and commented, "We villagers don't want any trouble from you Anglos."

Tia censured, "Aw, hell, Aunt Alicia, he isn't here to cause trouble. He is here to prevent it from happening."

Moving toward the stove, Alicia snapped, "Control your nasty talk, Tia. You have been around Anglos so much that you curse like them. Anglos bring trouble, not prevent it. You will see that I'm right." Alicia returned with a skillet.

Fargo watched her heap his plate with scrambled eggs and green chiles, then fill Tia's plate. Tia stood, stepped to the stove and brought back a stack of hot corn tortillas. Fargo rolled one around some of the eggs and poked half into his mouth.

Tia said, "The man that got away, maybe he went to Amado."

"It's possible," Fargo replied. "He could be most anywhere by now. I will ride to Amado tomorrow."

"Why not now?" Alicia suggested, a trace of hope in her tone.

"Because," Tia answered, and did not explain.

An older boy seated at the far end of the table across from Fargo said through a naughty grin, "Because Aunt Tia wants to teach him Aztec customs, that's why."

"Shut your mouth, Roberto," Alicia barked.

Tia laughed. The children giggled. Fargo focused on his eggs. After eating, Fargo excused himself from the table and said he needed to look in on his horse. He thanked Alicia for feeding him, then left.

Roberto appeared at the rails while Fargo had the dandy brush busy brushing the Ovaro's coat. For openers, Roberto said, "That's a pretty horse, *senor*. I've never seen one like that."

"He's a pinto stallion, called an Ovaro. After a rain, he fairly gleams."

Roberto changed the subject. "Aunt Tia likes you. I know she does from the way she looks at you. She likes Anglos, especially big ones like you. Are you going to wrestle her?"

Fargo asked himself if there was anything these villagers did not know. He changed the subject. "Roberto, what do you do to keep out of trouble all day?"

Roberto climbed over the rails and came to him before answering. "Pick beans and corn. I've never been to Tucson. What's it like?"

"You wouldn't like it. You belong right here, Roberto, where there is peace and tranquility."

"Uh, what does that mean?"

"No problems," Fargo suggested. "Tucson is a rough place. Believe me. You wouldn't fit in."

"Aunt Tia does."

"Your Aunt Tia is a woman. All women have a way of fitting in. Boys, especially Mexican boys, do not."

That wasn't good enough of an answer as far as Roberto was concerned. He said, "I'll go to Tucson when I grow up. Are you going to shoot that man when you find him?''

"Might. He stole my rifle, among other bad things he did.''

"I don't think he went to Amado.''

"Oh? Why not?'' Fargo stepped to his saddlebags and put the dandy brush in a pouch.

Roberto replied, "I've been to Amado. It's littler than our village. There isn't anywhere for him to hide in Amado.''

Fargo stepped over the top rail and headed for the cantina. When Roberto caught up with him, Fargo said, "That doesn't mean he hasn't been there. If he has, maybe somebody can tell me in which direction he went when he left.''

"Maybe. Are you going to the cantina?''

"Thought I would.''

"Mamasita hollered at Papa for taking me when I was little. I can look in, but I can't go until I'm bigger.''

"Listen to your mamasita.''

Roberto stopped just short of the door. As Fargo entered he rumpled the boy's hair. The aroma of coffee teased Fargo's nostrils the instant he stepped inside the saloon. Six men sat at two tables. Cups of coffee were in front of two, tequila in front of the other four. A seventh man stood at the bar, watching Hector fill a cup for him. Fargo smiled and nodded to the men. He went to Hector and asked, "Do you have enough for me in that coffeepot?''

Hector nodded and drew a cup to him. From the dark shadows in the back of the room, a chord was strummed on a guitar. Fargo turned and looked. A young man sat in the corner, near a tall stack of boxes. He strummed the same chord a second time, then rested the guitar on his lap and studied Fargo.

Fargo noticed all the men also studied him. Their grim expressions conveyed much concern, if not outright fear. Fargo felt his body tense. He turned to leave without drinking from the cup. Halfway to the door, Tia breezed through it, beaming a wide smile. The men's expressions instantly took a turn for the better. Their eyes seemed to twinkle at the sight of Tia. As they shifted in their chairs, they grinned and smiled.

Tia leaned the small of her back on the rim of the bar and said cheerily, ''That's more like I remember my uncles. Glum faces don't belong on any of my favorite men. Oscarito, did I hear you strum? Where are you, Oscarito?''

Oscar strummed again.

Fargo saw her remove castanets from her skirt pocket. She clicked them once, then sepped onto the seat of a chair at the table where four men sat. She paused to raise the hem of her skirt to her knees, then stepped on top of the table and smiled down at the men. Fargo went back and retrieved his cup of coffee.

Tia fluttered the hard wood shells and said, ''Make it passionate and fast, Oscarito.''

Oscar stood and started playing. After a few beats, Tia launched into a hip-bouncing, foot-stomping dance that excited her small audience. She put the castanets to work and encouraged the men to pick up on the beat. Tia gathered a handful of the front of her skirt and held it high as she twirled and danced a frenzied gypsy flamenco that bordered on wild abandon. As she danced, she loosened her braid of hair to flow free. Now her long hair became strands of whips that she ''snapped'' and ''cracked'' by lolling and jerking her head violently, all the while keeping the castanets clicking in rhythm with the guitar. When Oscar stopped playing abruptly, Tia dropped onto her knees and bowed her head to touch the table top. Fargo and all the men applauded.

Tia swiveled on her knees and kissed each man at the table on his forehead.

She said to all, "Stay happy, uncles. I go now to talk with this big Anglo. He's your friend, and mine, too."

Tia towed Fargo outside and said, "It will be too hot on the roof. We will sit in the shade under the shed and kiss till the sun goes down. *Si?*"

Fargo curled an arm around her waist and pulled her close to his side. On the way to the goat pen, Tia stopped to fetch an *olla* of drinking water from her aunt. Lying on a pile of hay under the shed, they drank from it. Then Fargo pulled her atop him and got comfortable. Their lips met. Tia's left hand moved to his nape, her right to his chest. Her breathing quickened. Fargo dipped his right hand inside her blouse and cupped the left breast. His left hand worked inside the waist of her skirt and moved down between her thighs. Tia began to squirm. Her hot tongue probed his mouth, fought passionately with his tongue. She moaned and hurried to open his fly.

"Wait, pretty Tia," he said. "We must wait 'till on the roof." He withdrew both his hands and peeled her fingers from him. "Children might see us," he explained.

"I don't care if they do."

"Well, honey, I do."

As though on cue, a little girl's voice asked, "Can I play on the hay with you?"

Fargo looked and saw the child peering between rails.

Tia muttered, "Aw, shit! It's little Esmerelda. She's a pest." In a stronger voice, Tia said, "Go home, Esmerelda. I think I hear your mama calling for you."

"I didn't hear her," Esmerelda said.

Fargo motioned her to come to him. Esmerelda climbed through the rails and slowly approached the pile of hay. Tia rolled off Fargo, sat and opened her arms to the bashful tot. "Come on, Esmerelda," Tia coaxed. "Let me hug you."

Glancing at Fargo, Tia mumbled, "He doesn't want to play with me."

Esmerelda ran and leaped into Tia's arms. After hugging and kissing the child, Tia lay her between them and told her, "Don't get friendly with him. He's mine."

Unsure, Esmerelda forced a smile at him. Fargo shot her a wink and pulled her next to him. Quiet now, warm and comfortable, one by one they drifted into sleep.

When they awakened shortly before sunset, Tia said, "Now, Esmerelda, you run along home. The Anglo and I have something to do. Something important."

Fargo leaned on the top rail and looked toward the cantina. Two men were entering, three leaving. When Esmerelda ran with outstretched arms to him, Fargo swung her high over the top rail and stood her gently on her feet. Esmerelda giggled, "That was fun. Do it again."

"No, Esmerelda," Tia began. "Once is enough. Now, go home."

Esmerelda picked up a pebble and threw it at Tia, then took off running. Fargo chuckled. Tia braced the top end of the ladder on the edge of the roof and scampered up it. Standing on the sod roof, she looked down at Fargo and said, "What are you waiting for, Anglo?"

Suddenly Robérto's voice came from the corridor below, "Psst! Psst! Aunt Tia, I know you are up there!"

All movement on the roof suddenly ceased. A frown on her face, Tia hissed, "Go away, Roberto! Now!"

Sensing the boy had more to say—his voice carried a trace of urgency—Fargo said, "What do you want, Roberto?"

"Papa sent me to tell you that four horsemen are coming from the north."

8

Fargo stood, faced north and scanned the terrain. Squinting, he mumbled, "Somebody has damn keen eyesight. I can hardly make them out." He continued to watch the four riders a few seconds to verify they were indeed headed toward Sahuarita. Turning to Tia, he said, "We'll finish this later."

He called down to the boy, "Roberto! Are you still there?"

"*Si!*"

"Go to the cantina. Tell everyone except Hector to go home and shut their doors and windows. Tell Hector to stay. Tell him Tia and I are coming. *Comprendo?*"

"*Si!*"

"*Vamoose.*"

Tia stood to dress. Looking north, she asked, "Trouble?"

"Could be," Fargo answered dryly. He pulled on his left boot and added, "My guess is they will come straight to the cantina."

"What if they are strangers? Strangers wouldn't know where to find the cantina."

"They will find it easy enough, because you, my sweet, will be standing just outside to greet them with a big smile."

"Oh? And where will you be?"

"Inside with Hector. I'll be behind that stack of boxes. Is there a back door?"

"*Si.* There is a small storeroom by the boxes. The door is back there. You will see it. What are you going to do?"

"If they are friendly, I will reveal myself. If they are hostile, I'll fight them. You engage them in conversation till we know their intention. Ready?"

Tia nodded. Fargo preceded her down the ladder, then held it steady for her. They hurried to the cantina. Fargo was surprised to find a crowd of peons inside. He said, "We have only a few minutes before the riders arrive. I will be behind the boxes. Don't give me away. Not one glance toward the boxes. I don't want them to know I'm listening. Act normal. Tia will draw their attention from just outside the front door. *Comprendo?*"

He watched them exchange nervous glances. Finally, Hector said, *"Senor*, we don't want any trouble." Hector's gaze lowered to the big Colt. "No shooting, *senor*."

Fargo hoped for the best. He nodded, then told Tia to step outside. He moved behind the boxes and told Hector, "Blow out all the lamps and candles except one. I want it dark back here."

As Hector extinguished the flames, Fargo rearranged the boxes, then opened the back door and looked out. Roberto stared at him. Fargo heard the horses approaching. It was too late to order Roberto to go home. Fargo said, "Roberto, run behind the houses to the shed. When it's safe, climb the ladder and hide on the roof. *Andale.*"

"Si," Roberto replied, then took off running.

Fargo left the door ajar and stepped to the boxes to wait. He watched Tia strike a sensuous pose as the horses drew near. Then he head Whip Bassett say, "Well, looky here, Pinky, a hot tamale if I ever saw one."

Tia quickly retreated to the bar. The riders dismounted and filed through the doorway, Whip first, then Bucky and Pinky. The man Fargo had seen carrying the saddle followed Pinky. All four moved to the bar and scanned the peons' faces. Fargo sensed they didn't come to Sahuarita to play.

Apparently Tia sensed it, too, for she asked, "Passing through, *amigos*?"

Pinky glanced at her. "Mebbe. Where did you learn to speak English?"

"From cowboys," she answered.

"Tell him we want whiskey," Pinky muttered.

"There is no whiskey, *senor*," Tia replied. "Only warm *cerveza* and tequila."

Whip looked straight at the boxes and asked, "What's back there?"

When Whip started walking toward the boxes, Fargo's gun hand went to the Colt's grip. Tia clicked the castanets. Whip halted. She said, "Nothing but junk, *senor*."

Pinky said, "We're looking for a big man riding a black-and-white horse. Has anybody seen him?"

"Why are you looking for him?" Tia inquired.

Fargo watched Pinky step to her. He grabbed a fistful of her blouse, yanked her close and snarled, "Don't give me any shit, bitch. Have you seen him?" He shoved her backward, into peons seated at the table.

Collecting herself, Tia gasped, "*Si, senor*. The man was here. He said he was lookin for a mean Anglo."

The fellow Fargo did not know stepped in front of Tia and growled, "Did he say who? Speak up or I will kill you here and now!"

Fargo drew the Colt.

Tia backed away and said, "No, *senor*. Only that the man had shot him during a gunfight in Tucson."

"That's Fargo, all right," Bucky said.

"Yeah," the man facing Tia agreed. "And he's looking for my paw." Pete Miller's gun hand shot to Tia's long hair and grabbed a handful of it. Pulling her face close to his, Pete hissed, "Is he still in Sahuarita? Don't lie."

Fargo thumbed back the hammer.

Tia gulped, then lied, "No, *senor*. He left about an hour ago."

"In which direction?" Pinky wanted to know.

Tia answered, "He rode east."

Pinky turned and asked Hector, "Is that right?"

Hector, sweat pumping from his forehead, shrugged and said, "*Mi no habla inglesa, senor.*"

"What do you think?" Whip asked Pete.

After a pause, Pete answered, "I think if we don't catch up to him, I'll come back and cut this skinny Mexican whore's throat for lying to me. Understand, bitch?"

"*Si, si, senor.*"

Pete flung her against the table, then strode outside, to his horse. The three gunslingers followed him. Pinky paused in the doorway, turned and warned Tia, "For your sake, and these men's, you better not be lying. If you are, we'll come back and shoot the whole lot of you."

Fargo watched him go outside, then eased the hammer down and holstered the Colt. He waited until he heard them ride away, then gestured for Hector to go out and check. He did and signaled all clear. Fargo stepped around the boxes and moved to the bar.

Mopping his brow with a bar rag, Hector allowed, "That was too close for me, *senor*. Those Anglos are bad. Tia, why did you lie? They will return and kill us."

"No, they won't kill you," Fargo began. "They will come back to Sahuarita, all right, but they won't hurt anyone, because you will tell them the truth. You will make them understand that Tia lied because I had a gun pointed at her head from behind the boxes. You will say that after they left, I took Tia and headed south. You can say that because it is the truth, and they will see it is so in your eyes." Fargo headed for the front door. Without looking back, he said, "Come on, Tia. We must hurry."

No more was said until they were at the goat pen. Fargo called up to the boy. "Roberto, are you still on the roof?"

Roberto appeared next to the ladder. "*Sí*. Can I come down? I'm scared. I want to go home."

"Hand down my bedding first."

Roberto pitched it down to him, then came down the ladder and ran down the corridor, without looking back. Fargo rolled and tied his bedroll.

Tia asked, "Do I ride the burro? She doesn't move so fast."

Stepping over the top rail, Fargo said, "No. We ride double." He moved to the Ovaro and started making him ready for the trail. When he finished, Tia lowered the rails so Fargo could lead the stallion out, then put them back in place. He extended a hand to her. Tia grabbed it, and he yanked her up to ride behind him.

Moments later he had the Ovaro headed south at a steady gallop. The ink-black night quickly swallowed Sahuarita from Fargo's sight. He reckoned if he couldn't see the village, neither could the gunmen. They wouldn't find it until daybreak. By that time he would be in Amado.

The Big Dipper hung in its twelve o'clock position when Tia announced, "There is a water hole ahead and slightly to the left."

Fargo slowed the pinto's pace and searched for the water hole. Tia pointed off to the left and said, "It's over that way, Fargo."

He was on it before he saw it and halted. The pool of spring-fed water was larger than he had imagined. Tia slipped to the ground and immediately started undressing. Fargo sat easy in the saddle and watched her dive into the pool.

Tia surfaced gasping, "*Madre Dio!* This water is cold!" Her teeth started to chatter. "Come on in with me."

Chuckling, Fargo dismounted. "I think I will wait to bathe

in Amado. They do have a place, don't they?'' He removed the bedroll and spread it near the edge of the pool, then sat on it to undress.

Tia swam for a short while before she left the icy water. Crawling onto the bedding, she stammered, ''I'm freezing.'' She dropped facedown next to him and snuggled close. Fargo closed the bedroll around both of them to quell her trembling. He lay on his back, looked at the stars. Neither spoke, but Tia held him tightly. Soon her grip relaxed. Fargo felt her slow, even breaths in the crook of his shoulder and knew she had found sleep. He shut his eyes and did the same.

A warm sun awakened him, but not Tia. During the night she had rolled her back to him. Fargo eased out of the bedroll and walked a short distance. Relieving himself, he looked at the landscape, pool, and sky. The barren terrain was dotted with barrel cactus, the pool stood tranquil, the sky filled with small cumulus clouds, not unlike a woman's powder puffs.

He returned to the bedroll and sat to dress. He nudged Tia awake and told her it was time to go.

Minutes later they were headed south again. They would eat in Amado.

Shortly before noon they rode into Amado. The village was smaller than Sahuarita, but not as compact. Here the adobe homes stood apart. There were no streets or corridors, just well-worn footpaths that meandered between the houses, sheds, and barns, all leading to the village well. A large corn-field, long since dried, stood just to the east of the village, and next to it a bean field, also dry.

Smiling children ran to greet them, then followed alongside the Ovaro. They chatted back and forth to Tia. ''Why are you riding on that Anglo horse, Tia?'' ''Did you bring me a present, Tia?'' ''Why were you gone so long, Tia?'' Their questions were endless. Smiling, laughing, Tia answered all of them.

"Where are we going?" Fargo asked.

Tia pointed to a home near the well.

Fargo rode to it, dismounted and helped Tia to the ground. A tall, slender, older woman appeared in the doorway, then came and embraced Tia. The woman suggested, "Put your horse in the barn behind the house, then come inside, *senor*."

A long shed, enclosed on three sides, was adjacent to the barn. Fargo pulled the barn door open and led the stallion inside. Gaps between the severely weathered planks allowed sunlight to filter in. Fargo relieved the Ovaro of his burden and set it on the ground next to a pile of hay. He looked at the flat roof and wondered why the wind had not blown it away. Not only was the roof flimsy, like the walls, it was also pocked with holes, some as large as his head. Passing next to the wall common with one end of the shed, he struck a board with a fist and broke it clean in two. "That was easy enough," he muttered, and peered through the new hole.

Gardening tools hung on the shed's rear wall. An anvil mounted on a free-standing stump stood in the middle of the shed, a circular whetstone, also on a stump was nearby. Leather and hides lay on a rickety table near the far end of the shed.

Fargo went to have a look at the leather. He found partially completed hand-tooled belts of intricate designs. He wrapped one around his waist.

A man's voice spoke from behind him, "It looks good on you, *senor*."

Fargo looked at the smiling man. The man was also unusually tall and much older than he, clean-shaven and bare-chested. Fargo reckoned the man was Tia's father. "Yes, it does," Fargo agreed. "Your work?"

"*Si*. It gives me something to do after our crops are harvested. My name is José Burciaga. You are?" He came closer and extended his right hand.

Taking it, Fargo replied, "Skye Fargo."

"My daughter said I would find a big Anglo and his horse in the barn. She didn't say you were tall. Neither did she say you have a pretty stallion. The belt is nearly finished. After it's done, I will give it to you for bringing Tia home."

To refuse, Fargo knew it would be an insult to José. Nonetheless, the craftsmanship of the belt, the many hours spent on it—Fargo said, "Thank you, José. I will pay you to make me a new saddle case for my rifle. Can do?"

"*Si*. I can make anything out of leather."

Fargo returned the belt to the table, then went to the barn and got his saddle case. Showing it to José, he said, "Same everything, except for a pattern of your choosing."

José inspected the saddle case. "I will make it out of black leather. How long will you be in Amado? Ten days?"

"No. I leave at daybreak. But I can come back for it. How much? I pay in advance."

"The belt and saddle case will be waiting for you. Five dollars?"

Fargo forced him to accept ten dollars. José quickly and expertly transferred the saddle case's dimensions onto a section of tanned leather, then handed the saddle case to Fargo. He walked with Fargo to the barn door, where he waited while the big man returned the saddle case to his other belongings.

Walking to the house, José said, "I didn't see your rifle."

"It's a long story that ends with a man stealing it. I'm determined to find him and get it back. That's why I am leaving at daybreak."

Nothing more was said until they were seated at the Burciaga's kitchen table. Sipping what Fargo considered extremely strong coffee, José said, "*Senor,* Arizona Territory is *mucho grande.* This man who stole your rifle, he could be anywhere."

"That's true," Fargo agreed. "But the last anyone saw of him, he was headed south. I reckoned he would keep going that way. The people in Sahuarita didn't see him."

Tia sat and said, "Before you ask, I have already. He didn't come to Amado. These people would have remembered if he did."

"Did you mention the four that showed up in Sahuarita?" Fargo quipped.

"God, no. Do you think—?"

Fargo cut in, "It's best to presume so."

"Presume what?" Tia's mother wondered aloud, fear of the unknown already appearing on her face and in her eyes.

Fargo shifted uneasily in his seat. He searched for words that would put her, all of them in the village, at ease, and found none. Now that the subject had been broached, he decided to level with Tia's parents, who would certainly spread the word. "Yesterday at sundown four Anglos rode into Sahuarita." He went on to explain he knew three of them and what happened in the cantina. As he spoke Tia's mother flicked nervous glances at her and crossed herself twice. José simply stared into his cup. "So, they are looking for me," Fargo concluded.

José quickly muttered, "And our daughter."

"*Si,*" his wife agreed, just as fast.

Tia made light of it. She smirked and said, "They are lost in the *deserto.* Besides, even if they find their way back to Sahuarita, they don't know where we are."

Fargo didn't believe it anymore than Tia did. He knew Pete Miller would dog them until he found them. Any man who would hire that trio of gunmen, he told himself, would finish what he started out to do.

Moreover, José obviously felt the same. He sighed heavily, then said, "No, daughter, these *hombres* are the kind that wer born to kill. They will not rest until they find and shoot you and *senor* Fargo. They will come to Amado."

His wife expressed her fears, "We are peaceful peons, Tia. You know that. We have no weapons to fight with. Child, we are at these men's mercy. The people of Sahuarita are frightened. You know they are. They will tell the men where to find you. Why, oh why, did you come here?"

José said, "What's done cannot be undone, Guadalupe. All we can do now is pray that the men do not come to Amado."

A brief silence followed José's sobering words. Finally Fargo spoke: "I don't intend to make Amado a battlefield. They are after me, not your people."

He wanted to say more, but Tia interrupted. "Suppose you are right. *If* they come, they will come from the north. Agreed?"

Fargo and José nodded.

Fargo cut her short. "What's the next village south of here?" He glanced at José.

Guadalupe answered, "Nogales."

"Why?" Tia asked.

"If Pedro doesn't see them by sundown," Fargo began, "it's safe to presume they halted at the water hole for the night. They would do that out of fear of missing Amado altogether during the night. And they will come to Amado. Regardless of when, Tia and I will not be here. Like I said, I don't intend to make Amado a battlefield. And that is what it would be. A bloody battleground. If there are no guns to contest them, they won't shoot. So, when they ride in you people tell them we have gone to Nogales. Tell them I mentioned I was searching for a man named Lester Miller.

Oh, yes, they will search all the homes and barns for me and Tia to make sure, but they won't hurt anyone. Then they will ride for Nogales. So by all means station Pedro on a rooftop.''

Rising, José said, "I'll tell little Pedro.'' He glanced at Guadalupe and added, "Come with me.'' It went without saying, José intended for his wife to help him spread the word that the villagers were in for bad trouble.

Fargo followed them as far as the front door. He saw the powder puff clouds had collected in the west. A rainstorm was inevitable.

Tia appeared beside him. She asked, "What are you thinking? Eh, big man?''

Fargo answered evenly, "I'm thinking Pedro will get wringing wet. I'm thinking Miller and his hired guns are also watching those clouds stack up. I'm thinking they—''

"We sleep in the barn tonight,'' Tia injected.

"In that sieve? We'll drown for sure.''

"No, we won't. It rarely rains in Amado.'' She shot him a wink and a smile.

Fargo chuckled.

And so it was. Pedro stood on a rooftop and scanned the northern horizon until darkness brought him down. The clouds roiled black and menacing, but so far shed not one raindrop. Silent lightning flashed continuously in them. The humid air was deathly still. No thunder rolled across the desert. Not one lamp or candle burned in all of Amado. The peons were afraid to light one for fear of guiding the terrible men to them. All but Tia and Fargo were cowering behind closed and barred doors and windows. Fargo and Tia lay naked on a pile of hay. The holes in the roof and walls allowed the flashes of lightning to light up the interior of the barn, much like a psychedelic display.

Fargo got up and ambled toward the barn door.

Panic-stricken, Tia bolted upright. "Where are you going? Come back, Fargo. You promised."

He didn't reply while going to the door. Fargo wanted to take the eager-for-sex female down a notch or two. Sex was all Tia had on her mind. If she wasn't talking about it, she was feeling him up. Swinging the door open, its hinges grated rather loudly. He said, "Calm down, honey. I'm just going outside to piss."

Fargo braced himself on the wall next to the door and started to relieve himself on the dry boards. A stiff breeze arose. Strong enough to swirl dust at his feet, move the door. Again the hinges squeaked. Fargo glanced skyward.

A man's voice snarled from behind him, "You caused my kid brother to get killed."

Fargo turned and flattened his back to the wall. Pete Miller sat astride a horse, aiming a big revolver at Fargo's broad chest. Pete had caught him naked and unarmed.

Pete growled, "*Adios,* you big son of a bitch."

9

In that instant, four things happened simultaneously; a massive bolt of lightning struck the roof of the shed and exploded; a hard wind slammed the barn door shut; an ear-splitting thunderclap shook the ground; and the bottom fell out of the clouds and unleashed a torrential downpour.

Miller's horse reared, tossed its head wildly, came down kicking, and twisting.

Miller fired.

Tia screamed.

The bullet tore through the board Fargo had pissed on.

The fierce wind held the door firmly shut. Fargo struggled to swing it open before Pete could get off another shot. The door handle broke loose. Fargo threw it at Miller.

Miller's spooked horse acted up, pawed the ground, backed, twisted, and snorted, making it difficult for Pete to fire.

Fargo began slamming his fists into the door, battering it down to get to his Colt inside.

Gunfire erupted within the village. Two different guns. Then three.

Pete Miller fired again. The slug missed Fargo's head by an inch, knocked a splintered hole in the plank.

Bucky Mullin's voice shouted, "Pinky! He's behind you!" A six-gun shot twice in rapid succession.

Pinky yelled, "Pete, we need help!"

The gunfire continued. Fargo had shattered a hole in the door large enough for him to squirm through. Half in and half out, he heard Miller shout, "I'll be back to kill you!"

Fargo ran to his gunbelt, withdrew the Colt, and raced back to the door. He forced it to swing out. Wind grabbed it and slammed it full open against the outer wall. The hinges broke loose. The wind carried the door away. Fargo stood in the opening and strained to see through the blinding rain and waited for lightning to flash. When it did, he didn't see Pete Miller. But he did hear gunfire.

He dashed to the rear of the Burciaga's house, plastered his back to it, then eased down its rough surface and looked around the corner. The shots came from the vicinity of the well. He stepped around the corner.

Pete's voice shouted, "Break off! We'll get the bastard later! Ride for the pond!"

Fargo fired once skyward to intimidate the gunslingers. Lightning flashed. He barely made out two riders as they sped past the well, headed north. Running to the well, he fired one bullet at the vanishing forms. The gunfire ended abruptly. Fargo heard two horses set in a dead-run head north. It was all over.

He sat on the well's edge and wondered who had challenged Miller's hired guns. The frightened villagers wouldn't have the spunk to do it, he reminded himself. Besides, there were no weapons in Amado. Fargo shouted, "Skye Fargo, here! I'm waiting at the well!"

He scanned through the wind-driven rain for the person. A flash of lightning caught a poncho-clad rider and horse punching through the deluge. The man rode toward him slowly, cautiously. Water spilled from all around the man's hat, making it impossible for Fargo to see his face. The fellow halted close to Fargo. He still could not make out the face.

"Mr. Fargo, are you all right?" the man asked.

"Well, I'll be shit!" Fargo eased off the well and stuck his hand out to Kid Ballas.

Taking it, Kid said, "You always go to a well buck naked in the night when it rains a gully-washer?"

"Sometimes, Kid. What brings you out on a stormy night like this?"

"I came to warn you they were coming."

Fargo gestured toward the unseen barn. "I'll lead you to my hideout."

Kid followed him to the barn. Fargo waved him inside, then stepped aside for Kid to ride through the dark rectangle. Kid dismounted. He looked at the leaking roof and said, "Don't do much good, does it?"

Walking to the bay, Fargo commented wryly, "It rarely rains in Amado."

Tia asked, "Can I come out now?"

Both men chuckled. Fargo answered, "Yes, Tia. Where are you, anyhow?"

"Under the hay," she said.

Groping for his clothes, Fargo told her to get dressed, that they were leaving. He sat on the hay and started pulling clothes on. "Kinda far from home, aren't you, sheriff?" Fargo remarked.

"I'm not the sheriff of Tucson anymore," Kid began.

Lightning flashed and lit up the barn's interior. Fargo saw him squatted next to his horse, staring out the doorway. Kid continued, "Pete Miller killed Raymond Simmons. Mildred Gibbons saw him do it."

Fargo reckoned he knew why, but he asked, anyhow.

Kid stood and moved to the doorway. Looking out, he explained, "Timothy and I were away at the time at Mr. Spivey's spread west of town. The next morning, Mildred told me all about what happened. According to her—and Doc subsequently verified part of it—Miller checked into the hotel and slept most of the day. Later, he came to the saloon and saw Glenn Bassett. To make a long story short, Miller said that he had received word from his kid brother that he and his father had found gold in Colorado, but cold weather ran them away before they could do anything about it. They went to Denver, where Pete's brother sent the telegram. Junior said they were going to Tucson. Pete was to meet them there. Lester Miller didn't know Junior had sent the message. Junior wanted Pete's apperance in Tucson to be a surprise for Lester. Pete went on to say Junior spoke in riddles about three men who needed to die because they knew too much."

"I suppose so," Fargo cut in, "specifically, where to find the gold next spring."

"That's what McCord said. Before he could say more, Doc told Pete you had killed three of them, Raymond one, and one got away. Doc didn't know he was telling Pete Miller who shot his kid brother. Nobody in the saloon except the gunslingers knew Pete Miller's name at the time. Then Doc left. Mildred and Raymond were alone with the four gunmen.

"Pete hired McCord, Mullins, and Bassett on the spot after he learned his father had escaped and you were searching for him with intent to kill. He got around to asking about how Junior died. Bassett told him. Pete drew his gun and shot Raymond four times."

"McCord suggested they ride south?" Fargo mused aloud. "That it, Kid?" He swung his gunbelt around his hips and buckled it on.

"Uh, huh," Kid answered. "Pinky said they should get out of Tucson now and start looking for you."

"Kid, Pinky said that because he didn't want to kill you."

"I know that, Mr. Fargo. What he doesn't know is, sooner or later you or I will shoot it out with him. Because Pete killed Raymond in my bailiwick, I want to be the one who gets him. You can have McCord and the others, but I want Pete Miller.''

Fargo nodded. ''If it works out that way, Kid. You ready to ride, Tia?''

''Of course,'' she answered.

Fargo began making the Ovaro ready for the trail. While putting on the bridle, he asked, ''Kid, what happened between you and Miss Katie? Are you going back for her?''

After a pause, Kid answered, ''Naw. It's all over between Kate and me. I'm not going back to Tucson. I gave my badge to Timothy. After this is over, I'm going back to Texas.''

Fargo handed Tia his poncho and told her to put it on, then he lifted her onto the stallion and headed for the doorway.

Mounting up, Kid asked, ''Have you figured out where Lester Miller went?''

Easing up into his saddle, Fargo admitted, ''Not yet. He wasn't seen in Sahuarita, and he didn't come here. Because he doesn't know about Junior's message, it follows he doesn't know about Pete being in the area. I reckon Lester Miller is down Mexico way for the winter. Tia, tell me again how far it is to Nogales.''

''On horseback? Oh, I guess about one day.''

Kid followed them out in the rain.

At daybreak, the wind layed. Shortly thereafter, the hard rain changed into a steady drizzle. The lightning and thunder had ceased, but the overcast sky remained. The horses plodded through rain soaked soil. Fargo wished it would end. He was eager to see Nogales appear on the horizon. He passed the time by chatting back and forth with Kid about Welsenburg and Kid's life on the ranch near Estelline, Texas.

Finally, the sun burned through the overcast and the drizzle slackened, then went away altogether. For a brief time they rode in comfortable weather, then the blazing sun turned the terrain into a sweltering torture chamber. The only good thing about last night's rainstorm was it erased their tracks. And nobody in Amado had seen them leave, so they couldn't say for sure in which direction they went. However, Fargo knew the crafty gunslingers would put two and two together soon enough and ride for Nogales.

Day gave way to night. Fargo halted long enough for the horses to rest while Roy and he made a small cooking fire to boil a pot of coffee and heat two tins of beans. After the trail meal, he and Kid covered the fire with sand, then they left.

At sunup Nogales loomed low on the horizon. An hour later they rode into the village. Tia suggested they go to the Catholic mission first thing. Fargo agreed, and Tia showed the way. The mission fronted a small *zocalo*. A paunchy priest stood in the entrance. Fargo and Tia dismounted at the foot of the steps. The priest came down to meet them.

The priest said, "Welcome to Nogales, my children." Then in the next breath, inquired rather suspiciously, "Why are you here?" He glanced at Tia, as though implying she should answer.

Fargo said, "Food, water, rest, and information, *padre*. And in that order."

The priest nodded. He glanced at Tia's head, then motioned for them to enter. Tia pulled a handkerchief from her skirt pocket and draped it over her head. Kid dismounted and followed Tia and Fargo inside. The priest brought up the rear. He commented, "We are poor people, so don't expect much in the way of a meal."

Walking toward the altar, Fargo noticed quite a number of fresh bullet holes in the adobe walls, but didn't ask about them.

The priest brushed past them. He and Tia knelt and quickly

crossed themselves. The priest rose and gestured for them to follow him. He led them to the back of the mission, to a small kitchen. A pot simmered on the stove. Fargo caught a whiff of bean soup. The priest gestured for them to sit at the small table. Fargo watched him remove three bowls from the cupboard, then ladle soup into each and serve them. He placed bread and a pitcher of water on the table, then stepped to the window and watched them eat.

Finally, the priest asked, "Where did you come from?"

"Amado," Tia answered. "And before that, Sahuarita."

"How long will you be here?" the priest quizzed.

The way he said it left Fargo with the impression the priest hoped to hear "not long." Fargo said, "The bullet holes in the sanctuary looked freshly made. What happened?"

The priest shrugged. "Bandits came to Nogales last week." He paused to put water cups on the table, then continued, "They were led by an Anglo."

Fargo and Kid stopped eating. They exchanged glances. Fargo said, "Oh? Describe the Anglo, *padre.*"

"He is a big man. Mean. His face, it looked like—"

"Biscuit dough," Fargo interrupted.

"Yes. How did you know?"

"Did he have a rifle?" Fargo pressed.

"They all had rifles."

"How many men were there?" Kid wanted to know.

"Counting the Anglo, thirteen," the priest began. "They shot four people, took what they wanted, and said they would come back."

Fargo asked, "Where did they go?"

"I don't know," the priest answered. "They rode south."

"Valle Verde?" Tia asked.

"It's possible," he replied.

"Thank you, *padre,* for the soup," Fargo said. "It was

tasty. You put the right amount of chile peppers in it for me. Is there a corral for our horses?"

"*Si*. When you leave go to your left. You will find it that way. How long will you be in Nogales?"

Standing, Fargo asked, "That makes twice you have asked the same question, *padre*. I get the idea you don't want us here. Is it because you think we will cause trouble?"

The single-minded priest opened his arms and hands and answered, "What do you want of us, *senor*?"

Fargo said, "Like I said, food, water, rest, and information. We leave tomorrow at dawn. In the meantime, we won't stir up any trouble. Is there a cantina?"

Fargo's words seemed to satisfy the priest. For the first time since they had met him, he smiled and said, "*Si,* we have a cantina. It's between here and the corral. You'll find it."

Kid and Tia stood, thanked the priest for the meal, then followed Fargo out of the mission. Walking their horses to the corral, Kid asked, "Do you reckon the Anglo is Lester Miller?"

Fargo nodded.

Tia groaned, "Poor Valle Verde."

"Tia, why don't you go to the cantina and tell everyone we're coming," Fargo said. He wanted to get a viewpoint of the bandits different from the *padre's*. Sending Tia ahead would prepare those in the cantina, put them at ease when he questioned them. "Tell them I want to talk about the bandits who attacked last week. Tell them not to be afraid of us. We mean them no harm."

Tia angled off and asked a small girl for directions to the cantina. The girl pointed but said nothing. Tia picked her up, told her to keep pointing the way.

The corral was in a large open area surrounded by rows of hovels on three sides. An old adobe building stood well away to the east. Nodding toward the structure, Fargo suggested they check it out as an alternate to the corral. He didn't want the banditos to spot the horses should they attack.

Up close he saw the entire roof had long since disappeared. The building was very old. The walls still stood, but even they were in various stages of crumbling. They led the horses inside and removed their saddles and other belongings. Then they wandered through the derelict building to familiarize themselves with its interior. Fargo went one way, Kid another.

Fargo found the old building quite spacious. He wondered what it was used for. Two long rows of columns spaced ten feet apart had obviouslsy formed a shady walkway. All doors leading to rooms from the colonaded arbor had long ago rotted and turned to dust. He looked into several rooms. The total absence of furniture and wall decor left him with no idea of what they might have been used for. He cut through a room. It opened into a long, wide patio that had a crumbling fountain in the middle. He stepped to the fountain and saw it still held water. Bubbles on the water's surface suggested a spring. He walked to the other side of the fountain and found where it overflowed through a missing hunk of its rim. A rivulet of water meandered through a doorway and disappeared.

Kid met him at the fountain. "Find anything interesting?" Fargo asked.

"It's ancient. Gives me the willies. But somebody uses it. I found two workrooms for making pottery. You?"

Fargo shook his head.

"They dug a hole to catch the water for the clay. I followed the flow to here."

"Might as well move our horses in here and let them water. We'll send somebody to feed them."

As he spoke, their horses wandered onto the patio and headed straight to the fountain.

"Come on, Kid. There's nothing left for us to do here."

They cut through the corral, went down a narrow, dusty street toward the *zocalo* in search of the cantina. A strumming guitar and the clicking of castanets led them to it. Inside they saw Tia dancing on the bar. Smiling peons looked on. The guitarist, one foot on the seat of a chair, watched as he played. Fargo and Kid waited in the doorway until the tune ended, then Fargo stepped to the bar and helped Tia down. The men applauded her, held their drinks in a toast of her. Tia curtsied and smiled hugely.

She said, "*Amigos,* these are the men I told you about." All eyes focused on Fargo and Kid. Tia continued, "The big man is Skye Fargo. The blushing man is Roy Ballas. They will ask you questions. Don't be afraid to answer." She glanced at Fargo.

He scanned their faces. Most were older men with eyes that appeared tired. Well, he thought, theirs was a hard life. He ordered a *cerveza*, then asked no one in particular, "You saw the *banditos*?"

A younger, wiry fellow having a long face and penetrating eyes muttered, "*Si,* we saw them. Why?"

Fargo detected a hint of animosity in the fellow's tone of voice. It resembled that of the priest's, but not as pronounced. Fargo shifted his gaze onto him. "Did you see the Anglo's rifle?" Fargo asked easy-like.

"I saw it," an older gentleman answered.

"Why?" the younger man asked.

Fargo ignored him. He stepped to where the old man sat at a table with three others. "Can you describe the rifle?" Fargo asked.

The old man described the Sharps.

Now it was definite. Odds were great that there weren't

two Sharps anywhere in these parts, certainly not south of the border. Cartridges for Sharps were scarce as hen's teeth. As best as he could tell, the butcher had taken five or six off him when he absconded with the weapon. Fargo kept the rifle fully loaded. If Lester had fired it, that meant he was running low on ammunition. Glancing among the men, Fargo posed the critical question, "Did the Anglo fire the rifle?"

He watched puzzled expressions form on the men's faces. Finally, the bartender offered, *"Senor,* there was a lot of shooting. We were too busy running away from them to know if he shot the rifle."

"Why?" the younger man asked.

Now Fargo turned to him. Rankled, he said, *"Amigo,* don't you know any word other than 'why'? But to answer you, this Anglo stole the rifle from me. He took only a handful of shells for it. He's got enough for twelve shots at best. So it's important for us to know his firepower. Did he have a revolver also?"

"Si," the bartender answered. "I saw it."

Fargo looked at Kid. "Kid, what do you think? Stay here and wait for them to come back, or go look for them?"

The priest answered from where he stood in heavy shadows near the back door, "Go look for them." He stepped from the shadows and continued, "These people don't want or need to see anymore senseless killing. And that is what will happen if you stay."

The sheriff in Kid rose to the surface. *"Padre,* it seems to make no difference if we stay or go," Kid began. "They will come back. You said so. When they do, they will shoot a few more of you people, even if we stay. I've fought men like them. As a gang, they're a crazed, bloodthirsty bunch. Left alone, they will keep on terrorizing you good people, take everything you have, and when there is no more, they will slaughter you just to see you bleed. Mr. Fargo and I may die in fighting them, but you can count on our guns taking a few with us. Maybe, just maybe, then they will leave you in peace."

The priest was unmoved by Kid's words. Walking to the front door, he said, "I want you to leave Nogales. Now." He went outside, turned and headed for the *zocalo*.

Tia said, "I think we should go to Valle Verde."

But Fargo only vaguely heard her because he was watching the long-faced man slip out the back door.

10

Fargo had the uneasy feeling that something was not as it should be. He moved into the shadows and opened the back door. Long Face was astride a bony all-white horse, racing like the wind, heading south. Fargo stared at him for a long moment before pulling the door shut. He went to Ballas and said, "Kid, you too tired to ride?"

"Not overly. What's on your mind?"

"That man had a horse out back. He rode away like the devil himself was chasing him. Headed south."

"It figures. You know, of course, he's gone to alert Miller and his gang of Mexico's worst."

Fargo nodded. "You got the feeling we're about to get between a rock and a hard place? Pete Miller coming from the north, Lester Miller from the south? Kid, that's seventeen guns."

Kid grinned. "I'll flip you to see who gets the odd one."

Fargo shared his grin. The young Texan was priceless. "Kid, never let it be said you were behind the door when God passed out guts."

"Just so I'll know not to shoot, what kind of horse does old man Miller ride? I've seen Pete's chestnut gelding."

Hell, Fargo mused, Kid's already carving out his share. "Gray dappled mare. What say you take on McCord and that bunch, too. I'll shoot it out with the dozen Mexican *banditos*."

"Mr. Fargo! Why that wouldn't be fair at all." Kid's eyes rolled back thoughtfully. "I'll trade you two hired guns for eight *banditos*."

Tia, her face a study of absolute bewilderment, proposed, "If I had a gun, I'd get two, maybe three."

"Can you fire a rifle?" Kid asked.

Tia promptly said, "*Si.*"

"Whoa!" Fargo grunted. "Leave her out of it. I want Lester Miller. Kid, you hold off the others till I get him, then I'll come help you."

"When do we leave?" Kid asked. "Where do we go?" he asked.

Fargo looked at Tia. "Tell me about Valle Verde."

"It is *muy bonita,*" Tia began. "In a long valley. Valle Verde is much larger than here. They have a stream and everything. The people are happy. I have girl cousins in Valle Verde." She glanced at Kid and smiled. "Six girl cousins," Tia added.

"How far?" Fargo asked.

"About four days," Tia replied.

Fargo stepped into the front doorway. He leaned on the framework and stared across the *calle* deep in thought.

Kid appeared behind him. "What are you thinking, Mr. Fargo?"

"Reasoning, Kid. Pete is about twenty-four hours behind us, his father four days ahead. It will take Long Face four days to get to Lester, four days for Lester and the *banditos* to get here. That means if we stay here, we can expect to fight Pete tomorrow, then Lester seven days later. I don't want to fight from here, Kid. I would rather meet them out in open country. I don't want to drag it out any longer than needed. So, we lead Pete south for a day, have it out with him, then meet Lester coming north three days later."

Kid nodded.

"Pete and that bunch—all seventeen of them for that matter—are accustomed to fighting in close quarters. Saloons and the like. Out in open country they would be like fish out of water. Nowhere to hide. So, we find flat, unobstructed terrain and dig in. They will see my black-and-white from a mile away and come straight to him. They'll be on us before they know it. We pop up, you get Pete and one other, I get the leavings. Then we ride south and do the same thing two or three days later." Fargo paused and gestured for Tia to join them.

"*Si?*" She stepped between them, into the street.

Fargo quizzed, "Tell us about the terrain between Nogales and Valle Verde. Is it flat? That sort of thing."

"For a long ways it is. There is nothing out there but cactus and the wind and dust devils. Why?"

"Borrow a shovel," he told her. "Meet us at the ruins by the corral. Come on, Kid, we need to pay the *padre* a short visit."

Coming to the *zocalo*, Fargo and Kid saw the priest talking with four women at the well. They angled for the group. One of the women noticed them coming and alerted the priest. He took a few paces toward the mission, then halted and looked at Fargo. When they got to him, the priest started walking again. He said, "Did you Anglos learn anything at the cantina?"

Fargo made it brief. "We are leaving for Valle Verde. Four bad men will be here in Nogales within twenty-four hours. They are looking for us to kill us. Tell them where we went and when we left. Do that and they won't hurt anyone." Fargo angled away from the mission steps and headed toward the ruins.

The priest caught Kid's shirt sleeve and asked, "Why did he tell me your destination?"

Kid brushed the priest's hand away, answered, "He has

153

already told you why. Do as he said." Kid spun and followed Fargo.

They had their horses ready to ride and all canteens filled when Tia appeared with the shovel. Kid poked the shovel's handle into the inner coil of his bedroll. They led the horses outside, mounted up, and rode away from Nogales shortly before high noon.

They rode the rest of the day and then all night, stopping only to rest their mounts. Once they made a small fire from desert growth, then left the ashes for Pete to find. Even before dawn Fargo knew they were where he wanted to be; the ground was flat as a pancake and cactus free.

The angry-red sun came up. With its appearance, Fargo saw buzzards circling low dead ahead. As he watched, they swooped down and landed. Then he saw a horse. At first he reckoned the eager buzzards were on hand, waiting for the animal to drop dead. Coming closer he and Kid saw differently. Several of the vultures picked on a human body.

Fargo pulled his neckerchief up over his nose as he came to the body—a man's—and dismounted. The buzzards hopped away a short distance and craned to watch him. They had already stripped away all bare flesh and were shredding the back of the man's shirt to get at that which it covered when they were interrupted. Fargo rolled the body over. "It's Long Face," he told the others.

Kid eased from his saddle and got the shovel. Fargo noticed the mare favored her right foreleg. He went to her, speaking in a calm voice, knowing what he would find before he touched her. He ran gentle hands down the leg and found it broken about midway between the knee and hoof. He made the old girl lay, drew his Colt, and put her out of her misery. It went without saying what had happened. Pure and simple, Fargo concluded, Long Face had driven the mare to the point of exhaustion. She stumbled and fell, broke the leg. During the fall, she threw him headlong over her neck and head. Long Face hit hard on the ground and broke his neck.

Kid dug a shallow grave, then they buried the body. Leaning on the shovel, Kid wiped his brow and said, "So much for warning Lester Miller. What next, Mr. Fargo?"

Fargo scanned the horizons. Finally, he answered, "This is as good a place as any for us to wait for Pete. After we catch our wind, we will dig trenches to fight from." He looked at Tia still astride the pinto. "Tia, do you really know how to aim and shoot a rifle?"

"*Si*. The cowboys taught me."

Fargo took the shovel from Kid. He walked a short distance north of the grave, then drew a ten yard line in the sand with the tip of the shovel's blade.

Kid and Tia came to him. Kid said, "How do you want the trench dug?"

"Deep enough that when we lie they won't see us. Go straight down along the line, then angle away toward the grave. Fling the sand to the wind. I don't want them to see a thing."

"They will see the horses, won't they?" Tia asked.

"But not us," Kid explained. "That will confuse them just long enough for us to rise out of the trench and get off the first shots."

"You're a couple of smart *bastardos*," Tia smirked. "Hand me that shovel, Fargo. I'll dig first. I'm a good digger."

Fargo handed her the shovel. He and Kid sat and watched her start the trench. After Tia had opened about a two-yard section, Fargo took over. Two hours later, Kid finished their trench. He told them to lie in it, that he would ride out in front until he couldn't see them to check on the range. He took the shovel with him and stuck it in the sand to mark the spot, then rode back to the trench.

Fargo sat and looked at the marker. Kid said, "I couldn't see either of you or the trench line from that distance. About forty yards, I'd say."

Fargo nodded.

Kid asked, "Where do you want our horses?"

"Straight back of the trench about forty yards. That distance will cause us to shoot to kill."

"That's for dang sure," Kid replied dryly. He glanced at Tia and explained, "Mr. Fargo is saying that if we don't, we won't need the horses because we're dead."

Tia gulped.

They waited under the baking sun for the four horsemen to appear in the heat waves and pirouetting dust devils. Sunset found them still waiting. Fargo had a decision to make. He scanned the northern horizon a final time before the sun went down, then said, "They should have showed by now. That can only mean one of two things; they wandered off course and missed us altogether, or they aren't coming. Regardless, we'll sleep till one of us wakes up, then we mount up and continue to Valle Verde. How does that sound to you two?"

"I'll go get the horses," Kid offered.

When Kid returned, Fargo gave his bedroll to Tia and told her to get into it, that he would sleep in the poncho. She mumbled a protest, but did as he said.

Two miserable days and nights later, Valle Verde came into view shortly after sunrise. Centered in the lush green valley the village's beauty stood out like a radiant jewel. Sunrays kissed off the yellow dome of the mission's bell tower and dominated the spectacular view. Twin low mountains rose ever so gently, one on either side of the village. The valley itself followed a lazy stream that glistened golden in the sunrays. The stream flowed north to south from somewhere unseen to Fargo's left. Tired though he was,

Fargo felt all of it was beautiful. For the first time since leaving Colorado, he felt he was home.

Kid said it all: "My gosh, to think that butcher is here, enjoying this paradise."

Fargo nodded, nudged the Ovaro to proceed.

They entered Valle Verde forty-five minutes later, while the mission bell tolled. Tia said, "The priest, Father Alonzo, is calling the people to mass."

Fargo halted at the first *casa* he came to. A man appeared in the doorway. He didn't look frightened. That was a good sign as far as Fargo was concerned. He asked, anyhow, *"Pardon, senor.* Do you know if there are any *Americanos* in Valle Verde?"

The man looked at Tia, then at Kid before answering, "No, *senor.* There was. He and the *banditos* left a week ago."

A woman appeared behind him. She eyed Tia unfavorably. "Tomas, we must hurry to mass. What do they want?"

"They are inquiring about the *Americanos* and the *banditos,"* Tomas told her.

"Where did they go?" Fargo continued.

The woman answered, bitterly, "We don't know. Back to hell, probably, where they belong. Come Tomas, or we will be late." She pushed around him and added, "Let them ask somebody else." She shot Tia a hard stare, then hurried down the *calle.*

Tomas shrugged, then ran to catch up with his wife.

Fargo swiveled to face Tia. "Do you want me to drop you off at the mission to attend mass? Kid and I will find a place for the horses, then meet you at the cantina. There is a cantina?"

"Si, to both questions. I will ask Father Alonzo for more information after mass."

Fargo followed a stream of people to the mission. Tia eased

down off the pinto, tied her kerchief to cover the top of her head, and melded into the crowd. As usual, the mission fronted the *zocalo*. And this one was a huge rectangle without a well in its center. Where a well would have been an elevated gazebo stood instead. Mexican tile, each piece twelve inches square, covered the ground of the *zocalo*.

The stream, wide and shallow, flowed past the edge of the *zocalo* opposite the mission. It gurgled over larger pebbles and rocks. Normally, women would be ankle-deep, washing clothes in the stream. But not now. They were attending mass.

Casas contained within eight-foot-tall adobe walls were at either end of the village square. Ribbons of glazed tile of colorful patterns decorated the walls. Wooden doors were in the archways spaced evenly in the walls. Each gave entrance to the *casa* beyond.

The roofs of the *casas* were easily seen. They were red tile, and peaked. Fargo had seen such layouts several years ago. He knew there would be a pretty courtyard on the far side of the walls.

He stopped a man hurrying to mass and asked where to find the stable or corral. The fellow paused long enough to point south. They rode south on a *calle* until they heard and smelled horses. The corral was at the south end of Valle Verde. Seven well-fed horses were inside. Curious, the horses came to the railings and watched the new arrivals. Several saddles rode a big and lengthy tree trunk laying on the ground outside the corral. Fargo and Kid added theirs to them, then went to find the cantina. They found it about midway between the corral and village square. The stream ran behind the cantina.

Fargo stepped into a cool, comfortable room. A burly, aproned man, obviously the bartender, if not owner of the watering hole, dozed where he slouched in a chair at one of the six tables. Fargo didn't disturb him. He went behind the bar in search of bourbon and found none. He had to settle for whiskey. Kid sat at a table jammed against a window in the front of the cantina. Fargo joined him. Neither spoke while they waited for Tia to return, or the barkeep to awaken. A half hour passed before the priest of the people passed beyond the window. Mass was over.

As though he somehow knew it was, the bartender stirred, smacked his lips, and tensed when he saw Fargo and Kid. But he recovered quickly. He moved into the doorway and looked out at the oncoming pedestrians. When the foot traffic thinned, he turned to Fargo and Kid and asked what brought them to Valle Verde.

Fargo fumbled a two-bit piece from a pocket and handed it to the fellow. The chap's eyes narrowed slightly. Fargo said, "We're waiting for Tia Burciaga. Know her?"

"*Si*, I know Tia . . . and her six cousins, and their *madre* and *padre*. Tia is back?" His eyes seemed to twinkle.

"Tia is attending mass," Fargo said. "She will be along any minute now." He held out his empty glass to the barman and told him to pour two fingers deep with whiskey.

The fellow went behind the bar. Out of the corner of his eyes, Fargo saw him bite the quarter to see if it was real.

Kid muttered, "Tia is here."

Tia walked in with a slightly older, but shapely woman. They were laughing. They breezed inside the cantina and came to stand at the table. Excited, Tia said, "Fargo, buy a bottle or two of tequila and come with us. We'll have a party!"

Fargo said, "Did you learn anything, Tia?"

"*Si*. But hurry. I'll tell you on the way . . . Conchita is one of my cousins. I met her and the others at mass. I'll take you to meet them. Like I said, we will have fun."

Fargo looked at Kid. Both men groaned. Fargo hedged, "Tia, I'm too tired to play."

"No you're not. You can sleep later, after. All you want."

Fargo shrugged at Kid, then both slowly rose.

Tia turned to the bartender. "Romero, two bottles of tequila, if you please." She withdrew her castanets and clicked them a few times for emphasis and to speed him up.

Fargo left a dollar on the table. He and Kid walked outside. The women followed shortly, each carrying a bottle. Both hooked their free arms into one of the men's. Fargo asked where they were going.

Tia said, "Behind the mission. You'll love it. You'll see."

They started walking toward the *zocalo*. Fargo said, "What did the *padre* have to say?"

Tia began, "Father Alonzo told me that Lester Miller took the *banditos* to a village east of here seven days ago. He told me Miller's headquarters is here in Valle Verde. They killed all the *federales* and occupied their building on the other side of the stream. You saw it?"

Fargo nodded.

Tia went on, "Pete Miller hasn't been here."

"How many *banditos,* Tia?" Kid asked.

"Thirteen. Fargo, Father Alonzo gave his approval for you and Kid to—how did he put it? Reduce their numbers? I think he was saying for you to kill the *bastardos.*"

"Did he say when he expected Miller to return?" Fargo inquired.

"No. Only that he would be back."

Kid asked, "How far to the village east of here?"

Conchita answered, "Two days."

"Well, then, we can expect them back most anytime," Kid observed.

Fargo nodded.

A wall much like the others Fargo had seen encompassed

a *casa* a short distance behind the mission. The only differences were the area the walls surrounded was larger, and the doorless archway was massive, easily accessible to a man riding a horse. Fargo knew at once where they were leading him and Kid.

Passing under the archway, Fargo saw a fountain in the spacious courtyard. Beyond the fountain stood a two level adobe *casa* painted white, trimmed in yellow. A red-tiled roof gave shade to the wide porch, which ran the full length of the front of the *casa*. The windows were gone. In two, young females rested their elbows on the sills. They smiled and waved to Tia and Conchita.

Fargo muttered wryly, "Kid, you ever been in a Mexican whorehouse?"

Kid offered that he had not.

Fargo said, "Well, pardner, you're about to step into one."

Four young, shapely women came out to greet them. Tia let go of Fargo's arm and ran up the steps to embrace them. Fargo paused on the porch, but Conchita towed Kid inside.

Finally, Tia introduced her cousins and suggested they go inside to start the party. Inside, Fargo found what he expected: couches and chairs arranged for conversation, a small bar, and stairs leading up to the whores' rooms. He didn't see Kid or Conchita anywhere. He slumped down in a chair. Tia pulled the cork in her bottle of tequila. It made a popping sound as it came out.

Fargo thought he heard a gun fire when it did. Tia apparently did, too. Her eyes kicked up, and she looked out a window. Fargo stood and stepped to the door. He heard horses hooves pounding into Valle Verde from the east. "Kid!" he shouted, "We have company coming!"

Kid answered from the stairs, "I heard them, too. Miller and the *banditos*?"

"Yeah. Who else?" Fargo drew his Colt, checked to make sure it was fully loaded.

All the women except Tia started screaming and fled up the stairs.

Kid handed Tia his Henry and a fistful of shells for it.

All three watched through the wide archway. Women ran to scoop up their young, then raced for safety. The *banditos* spilled around the walls, headed for the *zocalo*. Fargo didn't see Lester Miller among them. One of the *banditos*, a big fellow, wearing a big *sombrero* and *bandoleros* crisscrossed over his chest, rode into the archway and halted. Sitting easy in his saddle, he shouted toward the *casa*, "I am back, my beauties!" He slapped his reins on the horse's rump. The horse charged forward.

Fargo said, "Stand aside, Kid, and let him come in." He withdrew his Arkansas-toothpick and flattened his back to the wall next to the door.

Tia made it easier for Fargo. She handed Kid the rifle and opened the door and greeted the huge *bandito* with a smile.

Fargo heard the horse halt, then the *bandito* come up the steps to Tia. He picked her up and backed inside. Fargo tapped him on the shoulder. The man spun to face him. Fargo shot him a wink. The brute dropped Tia, drew his pistol. Fargo plunged the stiletto hilt deep into the big belly and twisted violently.

Stunned and already dying, the fellow dropped the pistol. Reeling, he pulled the knife from his gut and flung it to the tiled floor, then sank onto his knees. Clutching his fatal wound he looked at Fargo with a puzzled expression on his face, as though asking, "Where did you come from?" Then he slowly keeled forward.

Kid said, "One down, a dozen to go. What next, Mr. Fargo?"

No sooner said than a man shouted "Rodriguez! Lester wants you! *Andale!*"

Tia whispered, "There's two of them. They are walking to the house."

"Open the door for them," Fargo muttered. "Kid, get ready. Don't shoot unless you have to." Fargo pulled the dead *bandito* to the wall, retrieved his knife and poised it to strike.

The men halted on the porch. One said to Tia, "Tell Rodriguez to come out."

Tia replied, "Come on in. He's upstairs with Conchita."

Fargo heard a pistol cock, the same man snarl, "You lie. Rodriguez would not touch Conchita. What's going on here?"

Fargo gestured for Kid to wait.

Tia backed out the doorway, then darted to one side, out of the way of the two men, who raced inside with pistols drawn. They saw the blood on the floor, spun to face Fargo and Kid, too late. Fargo shot the one on the left, Kid the other.

Replacing the spent cartridge, Fargo suggested, "It's high time we leave this whorehouse. They heard the shots."

Kid handed Tia the Henry.

They followed Fargo to the archway, when he paused to peer around the side. He didn't see any *banditos*. Instead he saw Pete Miller and his hired guns riding across the *zocalo*. Fargo said, "Pete and his bunch are on the square."

"Good," Kid said. "Now we have them all together. It'll be like shooting fish in a barrel."

Fargo grunted, "Let's get it done and over. Remember, Kid, Lester is mine. Kid, you go around the right side of the mission. I'll take the left. Tia, you go through a back window and go to the entrance. If any of them are on the square, we start firing. If none are, then we wait till they come.'' Having given them their marching orders, Fargo stepped out and dashed to the left rear corner of the mission.

He waited until Kid got to the other corner and Tia went through a back window, then he eased along the wall and peeked around the corner. He saw half a dozen *banditos* gathered in the shade under the gazebo's roof. Fargo pulled back and slow-counted to ten. He heard the Henry bark, then Kid's Smith & Wesson. Fargo stepped around the corner and sprinted toward the gazebo. Three *banditos'* bodies tumbled over the gazebo's green and white decorative fencing, victims of the Henry and Smith & Wesson. One of the *banditos* took dead aim on Fargo and fired. The slug thudded into the mission wall behind him. Fargo shot on the run. The *bandito* tumbled backward.

The other two *banditos* vaulted the fencing and hit the ground running toward the stream. The Henry dropped one, Kid the other. Fargo ran to hunker on the safe side of the gazebo. He waved Tia and Kid forward, then quickly reloaded. Peering over the floor of the gazebo, he saw the other *banditos*, Lester, Pete, and the hired gunmen run out of the building beyond the stream, then scatter left and right.

Kid and Tia ran up and sat with their backs to the base of the gazebo.

Kid said, ''By my count we still have nine to go. Pete is with the four that ran to the right.''

Fargo nodded. ''He's yours.'' Fargo kicked a hole in the base of the gazebo, then used his hands to pry boards away and made a hole large enough for Tia to crawl through. ''Crawl in,'' he told her, ''and cover the front of the mission while I'm gone. Ready, Kid?''

Kid didn't hesitate. Fargo watched him run crouched toward the walls at the north end of the *zocalo*. Bullets ricocheted off the tile behind him.

Fargo ran toward the cantina. Slugs chased him all the way across the square.

Now began the cat-and-mouse game. As he hugged the front surface of homes and watched high and low for signs of movement, Fargo listened to the sporadic gunfire on the north end of the village. Lester, Bucky and three of the *banditos* were somewhere on Fargo's end of Valle Verde.

He saw the shadow of a man on a roof in front of him appear on the adobe across the *calle*. He halted, kept his eyes focused on the shadow. Suddenly it disappeared. The man, a *bandito,* lept from the roof. He landed on his feet, pivoted and aimed his pistol at Fargo.

The impact of Fargo's bullet in the *bandito*'s head knocked him backward, dead before he hit the dusty ground. Fargo stepped over the body, then quickened his pace. Approaching the cantina, Bucky Mullins dived through its front door, rolled and fired twice. Both rounds hit where Fargo would've been had he not crossed to the other side of the tight corridor. Fargo shot Bucky between the eyes and muttered, "This Colt's barrel isn't bent." He reloaded while running toward the corral.

The other two *banditos* stepped from the end of a row of connected homes. One swung his rifle up to fire, the other took pistol shots at Fargo. One slug nicked his hat, the other kicked up a plume of dust between his feet. Fargo shot him in the heart before he could cock off a third round. The rifleman ducked around the corner.

Fargo chased him through the corral. The *bandito* dove over the saddles and stayed lying on the ground behind the tree trunk.

A shot rang out.

The bullet splintered a top rail on the corral.

Fargo grabbed a roan mare's mane and swung up astride her. The mare bucked, kicked, twisted and turned as she moved around inside the corral. Through bouncing vision Fargo glimpsed Lester Miller aiming Fargo's Sharps at him. Miller fired twice, missed both times. The mare cleared the top rail by a foot, then started running, heading for the square. Fargo hung on. He slid off the mare well before she neared the square.

Reloading, he saw Kid come up the stream's bank. Kid saw him, too. Kid gave him a thumbs-up sign.

The unmistakable bark of the Sharps rent the silence.

Kid grabbed his leg and collapsed into the water.

Fargo darted forward in an all-out run.

The Henry fired. Lester yelped. Fargo swung around the corner in time to see Lester go through the front door of the mission. The Sharps lay on the tile between the gazebo and missions steps. He didn't stop to pick it up. In his peripheral vision, he saw Tia emerge from her hiding place.

Inside the sanctuary Fargo spotted Lester crouched behind the altar. Both men fired at the same time.

Fargo's hot lead knocked the butcher's revolver out of his hand.

Lester's bullet creased Fargo's upper left arm.

Lester ran through the opening of the bell tower.

Fargo shot at him, but missed. The bullet kissed off a wall inside the bell tower and whined. Fargo had him cornered now, and unarmed. He holstered the Colt and took his time going to the bell tower. Stone steps led up to the opening above which hung the bell. A thick hemp rope dangled from the bell to the floor where Fargo stood looking up. He didn't see Lester, but he knew he was up there. It was at least fifty feet to the ground, far enough to cripple a man for life, if not kill him.

Fargo shouted, "You're all mine, now, Lester! I'm coming up to strangle you to death with my bare hands!"

Lester called back, "I'm waiting!"

Fargo started up the steps. At the top, he peered over the rim of the circular opening. Lester stood in one of the four corners that formed graceful arches and on which the dome rested. The arches overlooked Valle Verde. Fargo stepped out of the opening and came around the huge brass bell to confront Lester. One of them would die. Fargo didn't reckon on dying. Not today. Certainly not at the hands of a butcher-devil like Lester Miller.

The dough-faced man broke a twisted grin, balled his hands, and snarled, "I should have carved your guts out when I found you lying in that mud puddle."

"You damn sure should have," Fargo replied flatly.

Lester lunged at him, but Fargo spun away, and slammed a fist against Lester's head.

Lester dropped to his knees, and shook his head.

Fargo drove a fist into Lester's face, then Lester grabbed him around the thighs.

Fargo pounded his shoulders.

Lester tried to rise. Fargo grabbed him by the throat and began squeezing and lifting Lester erect at the same time.

Lester pulled Fargo's Colt from the holster.

Fargo felt him do it. His hands came away from the throat to wrench the Colt from Lester's grip.

Lester fell backward in the nick of time.

Fargo dodged behind the bell just as Lester fired. The bullet pinged off the bell.

Fargo heard the Sharps fire. Lester grunted and the Colt clattered to the floor. Lester toppled out of the arch overlooking the *zocalo*. He plunged, screaming all the way down. Then, abrupt silence.

Fargo stepped to the arch and looked down. Lester's crumpled body lay on the *zocalo*. A wisp of gunsmoke curled out the Sharps' barrel. Tia held the rifle to her right shoulder. Kid limped toward her.

The three gathered at the gazebo.

Handing Fargo his Sharps, Tia commented, "Shoots pretty accurate. It had a hard kick, though. Hurt my shoulder."

"Well," Fargo said, "I'll have to kiss it and make it well." He turned to Kid and said, "Kid, you're not hurt. It's just a flesh wound. Come on. We'll go to *la casa* and doctor it."

Kid braced on Fargo all the way. Stretched out on Conchita's bed, surrounded by Tia and her cousins, Kid said, "Tell me once more the name of this town."

"Valley Verde," Tia replied.

"No, it isn't," Fargo mused aloud.

All the females squinted at him.

Fargo said through an easy grin, "Henceforth, it will be known as Gun Valley."

LOOKING FORWARD!

**The following is the opening
section from the next novel in the exciting
Trailsman series from Signet:**

THE TRAILSMAN #118
ARIZONA SLAUGHTER

*1859, the Santa Maria Mountains—
a land where Apaches lurked
behind every boulder, wealthy
Spaniards lived like kings,
and lone riders usually
became buzzard bait . . .*

The warm wind blowing stiffly from the west carried the sharp crack of the shot for over a mile.

A red hawk circling high over the rugged Santa Maria Mountains heard it and instinctively banked in the opposite direction.

A lone coyote padding up a steep slope heard it and paused to tilt its head and listen.

And a magnificent Ovaro, a black-and-white pinto stallion, heard the sound and pricked up its ears as it moved at a leisurely westward pace along the bank of the shallow Santa Maria River.

The big man astride the Ovaro also listened with interest to the distant shot. As a seasoned frontiersman, he easily estimated the distance, then pondered the possibilities, his lake-blue eyes narrowing. It could be a hunter, he reckoned. Or someone out practicing. But since he was miles from any settlement and in the heart of Apache territory, he suspected the shot might have more sinister implications.

Not that he felt any fear. Skye Fargo didn't regard danger as most men did; he relished it. To him, any danger was a challenge to be bested with either his Colt, Sharps rifle, boot knife, or bare knuckles if necessary. He thrived where many a man would cringe, and that was the reason, perhaps more than any other, that men had taken to speaking of him in awed tones around their campfires at night. Never cross the Trailsman, they would say, unless you're looking for a plot of earth six feet under.

Fargo urged the Ovaro into a gallop, his curiosity getting the better of his caution. He must be within ten miles of his destination, the *rancho* of Don Celestino Otero, and it occurred to him that his potential employer might be somehow involved.

The pinto's pounding hooves raised little clouds of dust as the stallion followed the narrow game trail bordering the river up a low rise.

Reining up, Fargo scanned the terrain ahead, a broad expanse of boulder strewn land between two mountains. He saw no one, detected no hint of movement, and clucked the stallion into a gallop again. If he figured it right, the shot had come from the narrow pass between the mountains.

Another shot suddenly confirmed his hunch. Seconds later, wholesale firing commenced, attended by faint, savage whoops.

There could be no doubt. Apaches were involved. Fargo rode hard toward the pass, the fringe on his buckskins flying in the wind. He threaded a path among the boulders, the stallion responding superbly, the sounds of the conflict growing steadily louder. It sounded like a raging battle was in progress.

The blistering afternoon sun brought beads of sweat to Fargo's brow, and he mopped his right sleeve across his forehead. His muscular body flowed smoothly with the motion of his mount, horse and rider as one. Soon he came to a clear tract. Beyond was a jumble of boulders, then the pass.

As Fargo crossed the level ground, his mind flashed back to the reason for his presence in these remote mountains few white men had ever seen. A week ago he had arrived in Tucson, tired and saddle sore, after leading a small wagon train all the way from Missouri. He'd looked forward to a few days of rest and relaxation, and then he would be back on the trail, heading north into the Rockies. But it wasn't in the cards.

The third morning of his Tucson stay a Spaniard had shown up at his hotel door and requested to speak with him. The man, one José Rojos, presented himself as the foreman for a wealthy rancher named Celestino Otero. For some time, a band of fierce Apaches had been harassing Otero mercilessly, and unless something was done soon the vast *rancho* would be ruined. Otero had sent his foreman to Tucson in the hope of securing the services of men willing to fight the dreaded Apaches on their own terms. There had been no takers, and Rojos was all set to leave and break the bad news to his *patron* when he heard Fargo was in town.

A grim smile touched Fargo's lips at the memory. If he possessed a shred of common sense he would have declined the offer. But the promise of a gold *peso* for every day he stayed on the job and the sheer challenge of it were too tempting to resist.

Preoccupied with his thoughts, Fargo didn't see the other rider until he was almost to the boulders. Suddenly an Indian burst into view. He hauled on the reins, his right hand sweeping to the Colt, and he had the revolver leveled, his thumb beginning to pull the hammer back, when he realized he'd be shooting an unarmed man.

Swaying precariously on a fine brown stallion, his head bowed and his chin touching his chest, an Apache warrior came straight toward the Trailsman. His arms dangled uselessly at his sides; if not for the pressure of his legs on the animal he would surely have fallen. Except for a leather loincloth and high moccasins, the sinewy warrior was naked, his skin bronzed by constant exposure to the sun, his long hair bound at the forehead with a strip of deer skin. The horse he rode drew up of its own accord within ten feet of the Ovaro.

Fargo slowly lowered the Colt. He saw a neat hole high on the left side of the warrior's chest. Blood flowed steadily from the wound, which might well prove fatal.

Unexpectedly, the Apache looked up, his pain filled eyes resting on the big man and taking Fargo's measure. The warrior's weathered features betrayed no hostility. He stared for all of ten seconds, then his eyelids fluttered and his chin sagged again.

The shooting in the pass had died off.

Holstering the Colt, Fargo moved closer to the stallion, noting the fine Spanish bridle and saddle its previous owner must have valued very highly. He went to reach for the drooping reins when more gunfire erupted ahead, punctuated by a sound that galvanized him into instant action—the high, piercing shriek of a terrified woman.

Once more the pinto displayed its wing-footed speed. Fargo craned his neck for a glimpse of the gap between the towering peaks. He came within a dozen yards of his destination and spied a fancy Spanish-style wagon overturned up ahead. Nearby were prone figures. Before he could identify them, he rode past a high boulder and a shadow swooped down from above.

A heavy body slammed into the big man's shoulders and sent him flying from the pinto. Fargo came down hard on his right side, rolling to the right at the moment of impact and clawing for his Colt. He rose to his knee at the same moment his attacker plowed into him again, knocking him onto his back.

In a twinkling an Apache was on his chest and lifting a knife for a death stroke.

Fargo reacted instinctively, his right fist crunching on the warrior's mouth, his left clamping on the man's knife arm. He rolled and heaved, flinging the dazed Apache from him, then rose, the Colt clearing leather as he uncoiled.

Undaunted, the Apache blinked once and charged again.

Magnified by the boulders, the blast of the Colt seemed to echo and reecho. The ball caught the warrior in the center of his forehead and flipped him backwards to lie still in the dirt. A small cloud of acrid gunsmoke hung in the still air between them.

There was no time or need for Fargo to check the body. Whirling, he ran to where the pinto had stopped almost at the edge of the pass, worried an Apache might reach his mount before he did. Sure enough, a lean warrior dashed from out of nowhere, a tomahawk in hand, and raced toward the Ovaro. Fargo shot the man on the run, hitting him in the left temple. In an ungainly swirl of limbs the Apache toppled.

Mayhem prevailed in the pass. Apaches and *vaqueros* were engaged in a furious fight, with half a dozen corpses from each side littering the ground. The Indians had taken cover in rocks on the south side while the *vaqueros* were in similar cover to the north. Rifles and pistols boomed. Arrows and a few lances streaked across the gap.

All of this Fargo took in as he grabbed the pinto's reins and pulled the horse into the welcome shelter of a boulder. He peered out again, taking stock, seeking targets to shoot. As near as he could tell, the Apache had ambushed a party of *vaqueros* on their way to the *rancho*. Apparently the gruesome stories of Apache atrocities related by José Rojos were true.

He saw a number of dead and wounded horses in the pass and frowned, hearing their frightened whinnies and wishing he could put them out of their misery. To his way of thinking, hurting a poor horse amounted to callous cruelty. He'd never met a horse he didn't like, which was more than he could say about most men.

A commotion in the rocks to the south arrested Fargo's

attention. Two warriors were in the process of hauling a woman of distinctly Spanish origin, who was kicking and clawing furiously, to the southwest. They evidently planned to spirit her back to their village.

The *vaqueros* on the north side of the pass realized her plight and mounted a concerted rescue attempt. Over a dozen men, all in wide-brimmed hats and leather chaps, many with beards and mustaches, sprinted toward the Indians, firing hastily and shouting curses at their enemies. Their valiant attempt proved futile as four of them were struck by arrows before they had gone a third of the way. The rest paused, their nerve shattered, still shooting wildly. Yet another *vaquero* died, screaming with a shaft through his chest, and the remainder broke for the north side and shelter.

Fargo watched the two warriors move farther away. The other Apaches were loosing more arrows to deter pursuit. Nodding, he swung into the saddle and headed to the southwest, using every available boulder to screen him from hostile eyes. If he paralleled the base of the mountain for a spell, he should be able to intercept the two Apaches and their captive out of sight of the rest of the band.

He hunched low over the pommel, glancing up at the side of the slope, occasionally spotting the threesome. The woman struggled tirelessly, and he found himself admiring her courage. Abruptly, twenty yards later, he lost sight of them.

Stopping, Fargo probed the rocks and scraggly brush, concerned they would elude him. Where the hell could they have gone? Moments later they reappeared, only all three were on horses. They raced to the south, angling down the mountain. Perfect, he reflected, grinning, and moved to cut them off at the base. The warriors were engrossed in keeping the woman between them while negotiating a narrow trail and had no inkling of his presence.

Fargo slanted toward them, going from cover to cover. Gunshots and yells indicated that the fight still raged in the pass. He came to a barren knoll that concealed him from the descending pair of Apaches, reined sharply to the right, and mentally ticked off a count of ten. Then, with his lips curled grimly and the Colt cocked in his right hand, he galloped up and over the knoll, intending to catch the warriors by surprise.

Instead, his own eyes widened at finding *another* pair of Apaches waiting thirty feet away at the bottom of the mountain for their companions, who along with the woman had another dozen yards to go. Both men spun their mounts at the sound of the pinto's arrival on the scene. Both voiced defiant cries and charged.

Talk about bad luck. Fargo had no choice but to meet them head-on. There was nowhere to take cover and running away never entered his head. He bore down on the two warriors at a full gallop. The Indian on the right carried a lance, the one on the left a bow. He shot the bowman first as the warrior was pulling the string back and barely glimpsed the man toppling to the earth as he shifted his aim to the second Apache and squeezed off another shot.

The Apache reeled but stayed on his animal. He lifted the slender spear on high. At a range of fifteen feet he couldn't miss, even though wounded.

Fargo thumbed off two quick blasts, the rolling motion of the Ovaro throwing his aim off a mite but both struck the onrushing warrior in the head and catapulted the Apache off his horse.

By this time the woman and her captors had reached the base of the mountain. One already had a shaft nocked to a stout bow, which he now let fly.

Fargo saw the archer fire and instantly swung low on the left side of the pinto, holding on with his right forearm looped around the pommel and his right leg draped over the stallion's back. The arrow flashed past overhead, narrowly missing the Ovaro. Had he still been sitting in the saddle the shaft would have entered his chest.

He hauled himself up and holstered the empty Colt while coming to a stop, then whipped the Sharps from its scabbard. Levering a round into the chamber he took deliberate aim, and a heartbeat before the Indian loosed another deadly shaft, he fired. The big rifle boomed, bucking against his shoulder, and the warrior fell, the arrow sailing into the nearby ground.

Fargo scanned the mountain and saw no other Apaches. The woman, a raven-haired beauty who appeared to be in her early twenties, regarded him in astonishment. He rode over to her and bestowed a friendly smile. ''Hello ma'am. *Buenas tardes, senorita.* The name is Skye Fargo. I strongly suggest we leave here while we can.''

Up close her soft features were incredibly lovely, her complexion flawless. Frank brown eyes regarded him with a mixture of curiosity and fear. Her brown blouse and long black skirt, both soiled with dirt, clung suggestively to her shapely figure. The blouse had been ripped in her struggle and partially exposed the swelling top of her left breast.

''Didn't you hear me, lady?'' Fargo reiterated. *''Habla ingles?* We've got to get out of here before more Apaches come.'' He moved a bit nearer, intending to lay a hand on her shoulder to snap her out of her daze.

Without warning, the tigress cupped her hands together and swept her arms in a vicious arc.

Taken unawares, Fargo was hit on the chin. The blow rocked him in the saddle, jamming his teeth together and making him see bright pinpoints of swirling light. The pinto shied and he tugged on the reins, getting the animal under control. When next he glanced at the woman she was heading to the southwest at top speed. ''Dammit,'' he groused under his breath, and took off in pursuit. For all he knew, she might blunder into another band of Apaches. He had to save her in spite of herself.